MW00880478

Pensioners' Paradise Immigration Card

Visitor

(photo)

name *Library Copy*

hometown *Hanscom*

birthday _____ age ___

destination _____

arrival date _____

sponsor _____

poem title _____

author _____

text: _____

_____

_____

_____

_____

_____

_____

(office use) approved by _____

walkie talkie? yes / no

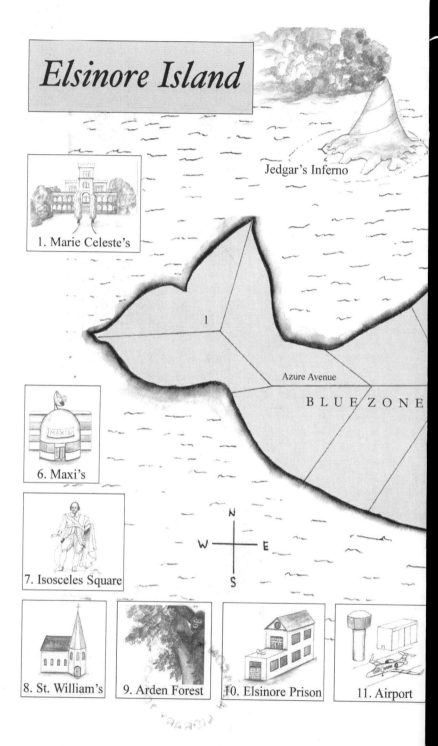

Elsinore Island

Jedgar's Inferno

1. Marie Celeste's

Azure Avenue

BLUE ZONE

6. Maxi's

7. Isosceles Square

8. St. William's

9. Arden Forest

10. Elsinore Prison

11. Airport

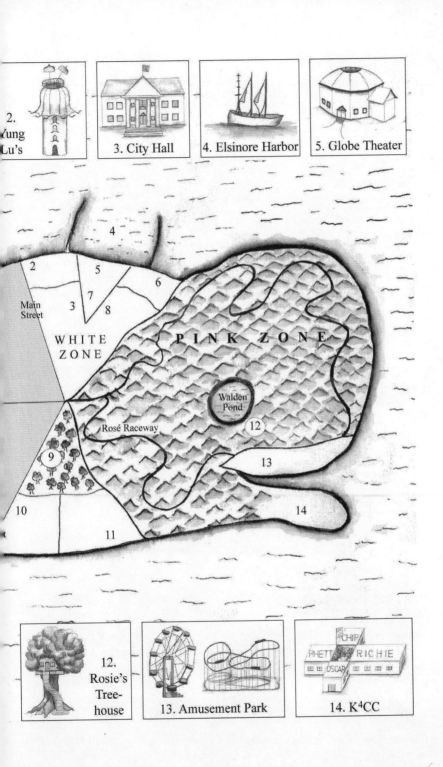

2.
Yung
Lu's

3. City Hall

4. Elsinore Harbor

5. Globe Theater

4

2

5

6

7

3

8

Main
Street

WHITE
ZONE

P I N K   Z O N E

Walden
Pond

12

Rosé Raceway

13

9

10

14

11

12. Rosie's Tree-house

13. Amusement Park

14. K⁴CC

CHIP

RHETT   RICHIE

OSCAR

William Shakespeare
1564–1616

Elizabeth Wahn

Lindsey
and The
Jedgar

Illustrated by Ivy Steele

Happy reading!
Elizabeth Wahn

Edizioni Il Labirinto

The original hardcover edition of this book was
published in 2005 by Il Labirinto.
For information regarding permission, write to
Il Labirinto, Via Leonori 67, 00147 Rome, Italy
labirinto@labirintolibri.com

First trade paperback edition: 2013
ISBN 978-1475282108
Printed in USA

Visit www.LindseyandtheJedgar.com

To Giovanni

I think he will carry this island home in his pocket...

WILLIAM SHAKESPEARE

CONTENTS

Chapter One

CRACK OF DAWN

Ryan Mandher hated to admit he was scared, but he was. He suspected that he was the only kid left on the island of Elsinore, and he had to find out what happened to the others.

Shortly before daybreak, he stole out of bed and tiptoed past his uncle's bedroom, down the staircase, and into the yard, cursing himself for ever having come. For the hundredth time, he asked himself why his uncle had wanted him to visit. The old guy seemed to hate him.

Behind the garage, Ryan found his bike lying in the shrubbery where he'd hidden it. He pulled it out and pedaled as fast as he could along the deserted streets. When he reached the airport, he looked around furtively and saw nobody.

Everything was eerily still. The planes, dark and watchful as crows, seemed to stare at him as he picked his way through the shadows to the in-and-out hatch. Finding the door unlocked, he slipped inside and opened the visitors' register. Through the window he spotted the immigration officer strolling down the runway toward him. He'd better hurry before she caught him snooping into her records.

Ryan's fingers trembled as he thumbed through the pages. In the section marked "July," he found his name in the middle of the list. The names above his had been crossed out with a thin black line — four boys, the ones he'd met the morning he arrived. Since then all four boys had disappeared.

Running his eyes down the page, he discovered the freshly-inked names of four newcomers scheduled to arrive. Much as he needed their help, he half wished he could warn them not to come. But there was nothing he could do. Not now. He quickly memorized the names of two boys from Washington, D.C., a girl from New Orleans, and a girl from San Diego, California.

With a shiver, Ryan noticed that the girl from California had a question mark by her name ... and her name was Lindsey O'Neill.

Chapter Two

FLIGHT OF FANTASY

Lindsey had never laid eyes on a plane like her great aunt's King Lear jet. It was electric blue, and the interior was furnished like a living room with a sofa and matching chairs, a fake fireplace, and a wide-angle movie screen. It's awesome, a flying sitcom set, she thought. I'm one lucky kid.

She hadn't wanted to go — she didn't even know her Great Aunt Marie – but as the engines began to purr with the promise of freedom, she was suddenly glad she was about to visit the old woman. What a way to run away from home!

Like Goldilocks poking around the three bears' house, she tested each seat before sinking into a leather armchair. She opened the instrument panel on the armrest, pressed a button to adjust her position, and felt herself gently rising. Another button swiveled her clockwise to face the window. She pushed a button that said "Rolling Massage" and her seat stretched out and began bouncing. When the novelty wore off, she hit "Halt" and settled into place for take-off.

A movie with the flight instructions came onto the screen, and then like magic she was airborne, looking down on the dwindling California coastline. As the plane cut through the sky, her spirits soared and her fears dissolved. Passing clouds slipped into gauze, and she could hardly believe that she was twenty-six thousand feet in the air heading to the South Seas.

The pilot's voice came over the intercom. "Everything all right, Lindsey?"

"Can I go talk to you?" she asked.

"Homesick already?" he chuckled. "Come on up."

The cockpit door swung open, and Lindsey sat down beside Captain Friedman.

The view of the Pacific Ocean was breathtaking, so bright that it hurt her eyes. Pinpoints of light shimmered like sequins forcing her to lower her gaze. A compass indicated that the plane was heading southwest, and she suddenly realized that every mile was taking her closer to Australia, the land of her dreams.

It had been over a week since her father had left home on an assignment to study wildlife in Australia, and Lindsey had been praying against all odds that she could go too. Now, with a private jet at her disposal, the dream seemed temptingly within reach, almost begging to materialize. Maybe if Australia wasn't too far out of the way, Captain Friedman could drop her off there. She pictured herself joining her dad on his visits to kangaroo habitats, and her imagination went wild.

Emboldened by hope, she took a deep breath and said, "I'd like to ask a very big favor."

"Fire away."

"Could you please take me to Sydney?"

"Australia! What's the matter? Cold feet? You're not having second thoughts about going to Pensioners' Paradise, are you?"

"No," she said. But she could have added, "Not anymore." She was ashamed to confess how panicky she'd been feeling, plagued by a zillion doubts, but that was a mind-frame ago.

With little idea what to expect, she had to admit that Pensioners' Paradise was beginning to seem quite promising, and she looked forward to spending the summer there. Even though pensioners were senior citizens, and Lindsey had never visited a retirement community, the term "paradise" raised expectations, and her aunt had assured her there'd be other kids vacationing there. Nevertheless, the choice between staying with an aunt in a retirement community or taking a safari with her dad in Australia had to be a no-brainer.

"You shouldn't listen to the things people say about Pensioners' Paradise," said the captain.

"What do they say?"

"Never you mind about that."

"Please tell me."

"Most people haven't heard of the place. We like our privacy. But it's nothing for you to worry about. You should be pretty safe."

"It's dangerous?" Once again Lindsey felt torn, wondering what she'd gotten herself into.

"Now don't go getting all worked up over nothing. Why do you want to go to Sydney?"

"My dad's there," she said. She was positive he'd be happy to see her. Every time he phoned, he'd say that he wished she could be with him. Would he be surprised when she suddenly showed up!

Come on, Captain Friedman, please, please, please say "Yes," she thought excitedly.

"I've got orders to take you to Pensioners' Paradise. Anyway, we don't have enough fuel to get to Australia."

Lindsey's face clouded. She turned her eyes away and inspected the flight panel, dozens of blinking lights and needles swinging back and forth on illuminated graph boards. To each side, the walls were plastered with pictures. Colorful snapshots of birds – doves, eagles, vultures, hawks, ravens, mockingbirds, and ostriches – were mounted on every spare inch of space. She spotted a framed photo of Captain Friedman sitting in the pilot's seat with a rooster on his lap. It was autographed "Sam Friedman and his best friend in the cockpit."

"Now you know why we call it a *cock*pit," he chortled. "Finest navigator I ever had."

Very funny, she thought moodily.

Directly beneath them an ocean liner looked no larger than a hazelnut pasted on a mat. Only the two parallel white strings in its wake gave a sense of motion.

"So, you'll be staying with your great aunt?" asked the captain. "What's she like?"

Sifting through new ideas, Lindsey began to worry that something might be wrong with the old woman.

"You've never met her?"

She shook her head. She wished she'd asked her dad more

questions. But then he always thought the best of everybody even his yucky girlfriends.

"Pillar of the community. A bit dotty about politics," said Captain Friedman.

"She's dying?"

"Good grief, no. She's still quite young."

Lindsey breathed a sigh of relief. "How old is she?"

"Early seventies, I'd guess."

"That isn't young."

"It is on Pensioners' Paradise. How old do you think I am?"

She looked him over. His face was tanned but not particularly wrinkled. He had a full head of hair graying at the temples. Under his short-sleeved uniform, his arms were lean and muscular.

"Dunno."

"Come on, guess."

She hated it when adults put her on the spot.

"Maybe thirty-five?"

Captain Friedman laughed merrily. "I'm eighty-nine."

"Eighty-nine years old?"

Whoa! He couldn't be serious? Nobody that old would be allowed to fly a plane – and with no co-pilot? What if he had a heart attack or something? Lindsey had learned some CPR at Girl Scouts, but she doubted she could save a full-grown man, and she certainly couldn't fly the plane. She looked out at the ocean. It was a very long way down.

"How old do people get?"

"The last time I checked, the life expectancy was around a hundred and thirty-five, but it's rising every year."

"You mean some of them are actually a hundred and thirty-five years old?" She gave him a long, hard look, and he nodded complacently.

"Most are younger. Some older. The oldest person there is Juanita Shringapur. She won't admit it, but she's a hundred and fifty-three. Still a good-looking gal even though she's past her prime."

Lindsey mulled it over and came to the conclusion that he was teasing her — like her sixth grade teacher who used to think he was so clever, always telling tall stories with a deadpan look on his face. In her opinion practical jokers were pretty dumb, but with nobody else to talk to she might as well play along.

"Why do they live so long?"

"It's the water. Montezuma's Miracle Mineral water, we call it. It springs from wells deep under the earth's surface. Does wonders. It can make you feel a bit lightheaded, so some people like your aunt prefer to boil it. She's the serious type. Wants to 'age gracefully,' says she."

"What happens if I drink it? I turn into a two-year-old or something?"

"Forgot to pack your diapers?" He broke into a toothy grin. "Not to worry. All it does is spry up your body cells. Keeps you right healthy. Ever hear of the Hayflick Limit?"

"No."

"It determines life expectancy. It's programmed into your genes just like hair color and all that. You can live on and on if you get around the Hayflick Limit. Montezuma water does that."

Lindsey was far from convinced. She tried to piece together the short conversations she'd had with her aunt – not a whole lot to go on.

"If she isn't dying, how come she said it might be my last chance to visit her?"

"How old are you?"

"Twelve."

"Well, nobody over twelve or under seventy is allowed on the islands."

"Really? There's lots of kids my age?"

"Maybe a couple of dozen summer visitors, but most of them won't be on Elsinore."

"What's Elsinore?"

"The capital. Largest island in the archipelago. That's where you're heading."

Tired of playing games, she dismissed most of his chatter, rubbed her eyes, and yawned.

"Why not get yourself a little shut-eye?" he said. "We've got a long trip ahead."

"You're doing it all yourself? No co-pilot?"

"In the closet booting up for the cruise." He indicated a door behind him. "During the cruise, I snooze."

Sure, she thought, he's a riot – like that wise crack about the rooster in the cockpit. He probably expects me to open the door so he can laugh his head off.

She was curious to take a peek, but she wasn't about to give him the satisfaction.

"If you want a movie, Alfred Hitchcock's classic *The Birds* is on channel one. My favorite. Thought you might enjoy it. The others are listed alphabetically on the remote. And help yourself to anything you want to eat. Food's in the fridge. Sofa bed's made up, and you'll find pillows in the linen closet, the one with a bluebird painted on the door. I'll call you an hour or so before we land."

"Goodnight, Captain Friedman," she said even though sunshine was pouring through the window like a good omen.

"Nighty-night," he said, shutting the door behind her.

*

While the King Lear jet streaked across a sparkling blue sky, on the other side of the Pacific, thousands of miles away, night still girded the islands of Pensioners' Paradise. Wide awake, adrift on a sea of troubles, eleven-year-old Ryan Mandher gazed from his bedroom window at an ocean flat and somber as a gravestone.

Cloaked in darkness, the whale-shaped island of Elsinore hid untold secrets. Ryan's thoughts wandered back to the girl named Lindsey, one more question mark in a flood of questions.

Ryan heard noises. He leaned out and saw two figures, his uncle and another man conversing in hushed tones. When they turned their heads in his direction, Ryan caught the word "helpless" or maybe it was "hopeless." Were they talking about him? As their voices faded, Ryan cast his eyes across the waters to a distant volcano and felt utterly alone.

Chapter Three

TOWARD DANGER

Lindsey awoke to the sound of Captain Friedman crooning his own homemade rap on the intercom:

> *The morning is a-breakin',*
> *And it's time to get you wakin'.*
> *We'll be landing in an hour.*
> *You've got time to take a shower.*
> *If your hungry belly's achin',*
> *Breakfast's in the makin' ...*

She rolled over to switch off her clock radio and slapped the air before realizing she wasn't home anymore. She was on a plane, all by herself, listening to the pilot's wake-up call. It seemed too good to be true.

She pinched herself. Yes, she was really on her way to Paradise – the sapphire of the South Seas as her great aunt called it. Lindsey pictured herself on a glorious tropical island, making new friends, and doing whatever she pleased while her sweet little old auntie baked cookies or sat knitting in a rocking chair.

As she got her bearings, Lindsey started remembering the stupid stuff that the captain had told her, but she didn't feel like dwelling on downers. Why worry when everything around her looked so solid and homey and welcoming?

So what if the pilot's an oddball, she mused. He probably means well, and the owner of a jet like this has got to be a kindhearted person.

With the adrenaline rushing through her veins, Lindsey

tucked away her misgivings and began working herself into a state of genuine enthusiasm. Giddy with anticipation, she showered, blew her hair dry, and rummaged through her suitcase looking for an outfit suitable for meeting a pillar of the community.

"Lindsey, there's some turbulence ahead," came the Captain's voice. "Better sit down and fasten your seatbelt until the warning sign stops flashing."

She pitched herself into a leather armchair, accidentally touched "Rolling Massage" with her elbow, and the seat started bouncing. In her confusion, she pressed the "High" button instead of the "Halt," and the bouncing got wilder. WHAP! – WHAP! – WHAP! The seat was dealing out a spanking.

"Yikes!" she cried, bumping her nose against a flower pot. Bobbing around out of control, she couldn't read the instrument panel, and she randomly punched one button after another. The seat flattened out and dropped to the floor. Hoping that Captain Friedman hadn't witnessed her embarrassing little performance, she struggled to her feet just as the fasten seatbelt sign turned off.

Thoughts of breakfast led her to the kitchenette. Behind the doors of a cabinet she discovered a refrigerator stocked with pudding and other soft foods – nothing solid to eat like an apple or a cracker.

Maybe my aunt has no teeth, she thought.

A panel inside the door listed the available drinks. She pressed the orange juice button, and four plump oranges rolled down a spout to be sliced in half by a miniature guillotine, squeezed to a froth, and poured into a tall glass, which she raised to her lips to toast her lucky day.

Unable to contain her excitement, she burst into the cockpit carrying her juice with her.

"Morning, little girl. Aren't you a treat for sore eyes? Pretty as a picture," said Captain Friedman.

She caught sight of herself in the overhead mirror. Her straight chestnut-red hair was shiny and neatly parted in the middle. She guessed she looked all right.

"You think my aunt will like me?"

"Of course. Anybody would fall for those dimples of yours," he smiled. "Want some breakfast? There's nice hot oatmeal."

"I'll just have juice." She'd sooner go hungry than eat oatmeal. She pulled out her cell phone and said, "Can I call my dad?"

"Here, use this," said the captain, and he passed her a banana-shaped instrument.

As she dialed he put on a headset, giving her the illusion of privacy.

She heard her father's voice, "Hey, Globe-trotter!"

Despite the nickname, Lindsey was no globe-trotter – she'd rarely set foot outside California. If anything, she was a wannabe traveler who usually got stuck home with live-in sitters whenever her father had to leave town on assignments. But not this time. The unexpected invitation from her great aunt had provided an escape hatch. Good old auntie had even sent a private jet, which was pretty mind-boggling. And Lindsey was ripe for adventure.

"Hey, Dad," she said, "you ever been on this plane? It looks like our living room only fancier."

"The blue King Lear jet –"

"With a fireplace and a chimney –"

"In case Santa drops in?" he laughed.

"And there's some kind of vibrating thing on the seats."

"It's supposed to ease muscle sores on long trips."

"And all the potted plants nailed to the window sills. My aunt's weird or something? Come on, tell me."

Her father said, "When you're as rich as your aunt is, you're considered eccentric not weird. But don't worry, she's a very particular lady, and that plane you're on is probably as safe as Air Force One."

"But she's kind of nutty, huh?" The aunt had sounded pretty normal on the phone, but Lindsey couldn't be sure.

"All O'Neills are kind of nutty except me, of course."

"And me!"

"By the way," he said, "Tiffany says you're to wear a dress."

"A dress!"

"To make a good impression. She put one in your suitcase."

"I *have* to?"

21

"Listen, honey, I don't feel like arguing. I'm counting on you to behave. Remember what I told you: any trouble, no dog."

Fat chance she'd forget! Lindsey sorely wanted a dog, and she had to keep out of trouble or he wouldn't get her one. Ever since he put her on summer probation, she'd been behaving like a perfect goodie-goodie, even pretending she could stand Tiffany.

"I'll practice saying, 'Yes, Aunt Marie.'"

"That's not what I meant. And be sure to call her Aunt Marie Celeste. She doesn't want anybody to mix her up with your other Aunt Marie. Give her my love and have a great time. I'm missing you bad, so keep in touch."

"Love you, Dad."

"Love you too."

Imagine his bothering about anything as stupid as a dress. The last thing he ever thought about was clothes. He was probably just trying to be a good parent. He was the only parent she had, and in Lindsey's opinion he was tops. She just wished he'd get rid of his girlfriends. It seemed like every bimbo in California was after him. But Tiffany was the worst.

If only my mom hadn't died, thought Lindsey, things would be different.

Try as she might, Lindsey couldn't remember her mother, but she felt close to her. Her mother had filled the house with her work – pictures, journals, albums of clippings, piles of unfinished manuscripts, and even a short book she'd written. They were now wrapped in brown paper and hidden in the recesses of a closet, but Lindsey had gone through them over and over again like a secret treasure trove. Sometimes it made her sad … sad for her father, sad for herself. But Lindsey wasn't much into self pity.

I'm going to have the best summer vacation in the whole wide world, she told herself, thanks to good old Aunt Marie … um … Aunt Marie Celeste!

"I'll be right back," she said to Captain Friedman as she popped out of her seat to go change her clothes.

Between layers of sports gear she came across her linen sundress, a trifle wrinkled and so old that she wasn't sure it would fit anymore, but she figured she'd better wear it. She tossed it

on, stepped into a pair of sandals, and raced back into the cockpit.
"Fasten your seatbelt and look out the window," said the captain. "Over there to the left."
She peered out toward the horizon.
"See anything?" he asked.
In the distance she could distinguish a cluster of brown lumps on the ocean. They looked like prehistoric anthills floating on the waves.
"Those are the islands?"
"Sure enough. We've made really good time. Strong tailwind. We'll be landing way ahead of schedule. I hope your robot's at the airport."
Not again! His sense of humor was wearing thin.
"My robot?" she said.
"Uh-huh. They do most of the work on Paradise. One of them will drive you to Marie Celeste's."
"Real robots? Like the *Star Wars* movie?"
"Nope. They don't look anything like that. They come in all sorts of shapes and sizes. Personalized engineering is our motto. Or animalized. Some of the robots look like teddy bears and whatever. Makes them seem more friendly-like."
"They aren't friendly?"
"They do what they're programmed to do," he said evenly. "Like my co-pilot."
She'd had enough. She jumped up and threw open the closet door. Doubled over and hunched against the wall was a life-sized, plastic doll dressed in a pilot's uniform. Lindsey nearly collapsed. She rolled back into her seat and caught her breath.
The jet dipped through the clouds and kept dropping altitude. The blue of the ocean softened into turquoise shallows, pearly and luminous as upturned shells, and the brown islands began to look greener. Coral reefs braceleted the smaller ones.
"Aw, naw," groaned Captain Friedman.
A series of shock waves hit the plane. It trembled as it bucked the air currents.
"What's wrong?" she gasped.
"Over to your right," he said, angrily punching the buttons on the flight panel.

She followed his eyes and spotted a pewter gray island with a rugged shore line and no hint of vegetation. A volcano loomed over it belching balloons of black smoke. It was so big that she had to crane her neck to see the top. Red-hot sparks burst from its monstrous mouth, and patches of pitch cut into the visibility. The tiny particles splattered the windshield like gnats on a summer night.

"It's going to erupt?"

"Mount Cinderella? Let's hope not. Drat that Jedgar," he muttered. "Up to the same old tricks."

"What's a Jedgar?"

"Better switch on the emergency radar."

As they cruised toward the whale-shaped island of Elsinore, the air began to clear, and she could pick out splashes of flame-colored flamboyant trees and lush palms hugging hills that swept into white, sandy beaches.

"What's a Jedgar?"

"Listen to me, little girl, don't you go telling your aunt that I mentioned the Jedgar. Do you want me to lose my job?"

"Captain Friedman, I'm not trying to be difficult or anything," she said, visibly shaken. "I mean, I couldn't care less about living to be a hundred and thirty-five, but I'd kind of like to see my thirteenth birthday."

He gently took her shoulders, turned her around to face him, and looked her in the eye.

"I'm afraid I've given you the wrong impression. There's nothing for you to fret over. Mount Cinderella's been around for a long time, and nobody's ever been hurt. You believe me, don't you?"

"I guess."

"Now give me a smile and don't go troubling yourself any more. I'll make a bargain with you. You keep quiet about the J-word, and I'll try to find a way to fly you to Australia. All right?"

There didn't seem to be much choice.

"Mmmm," she said.

It was more of a moan than an answer.

Chapter Four

ROBOTS
AND RUDE RELATIONS

Lindsey couldn't believe how small the airport was – smaller than a gas station. Captain Friedman taxied by it and continued down the runway past a line of private jets, helicopters, blimps, and gliders, and he neatly pulled into formation.

The airfield was astir. Crews of odd-looking workmen in overalls were unloading cargo from an airbus labeled "Out-Sourcing Supply Company." Shaggy, muscle-bound, and squat, they seemed more like trolls than humans.

"Who are they?" she asked.

"Robots," he said, opening the door for her. "You can hop out and go to immigration. I'll get your luggage."

She glanced around warily, but the creatures took no notice of her. Now that she was on land again, she began to feel more like her usual self. A warm, salty breeze rose from the sea, giving her a sense of normalcy – it smelled like southern California. She filled her lungs and followed the signs to the in-and-out hatch.

The immigration officer, a pert old woman dressed in a leotard with a ruffled tutu, perched like a white-haired ballerina on the edge of a desk. Despite the outlandish costume, she had a grandmotherly air about her. At the sight of Lindsey, she popped to her feet.

"Welcome to Elsinore. I suppose you're Lindsey O'Neill – from San Diego, California," she added uncertainly, as if expecting dozens of Lindsey O'Neills to show up at any moment.

Lindsey was thunderstruck. "I just remembered I haven't got a passport. I can't prove who I am."

"No need. We know who you are." She inspected Lindsey. "You're not over twelve, are you?"

"I just turned twelve."

"Then what are you waiting for? Recite your poem."

"Poem?"

"Nobody told you? It's the law. Gotta be able to recite a poem to get through immigration. Otherwise we're sending you back."

"What kind of poem?"

"Any poem will do, but if it's Shakespeare, you're entitled to a free walkie-talkie. Kind of like a cell phone but easier to use. Some of our older residents have trouble figuring out complicated technology, so we've devised all types of high-tech, low-brow Simple-Simon-System instruments."

"Oh."

"I'm still waiting to hear your poem."

Lindsey's mind went blank. She wrinkled her forehead and wracked her brain trying to remember a few lines from her part in the school play, Shakespeare's *A Midsummer-Night's Dream*. She hadn't thought about it for months and had almost forgotten it. Suddenly her expression cleared and she began to recite some verses:

> Over hill, over dale,
>   Through brush, through brier,
> Over park, over pale,
>   Through flood, through fire:
> I do wander everywhere …

"Hurray! I knew you could do it. You're officially here. Better tell the folks at home," she said, passing Lindsey a landline.

Lindsey took the phone and left a message on her dad's voice mail. When she finished, the woman handed her a small package.

Inside it Lindsey found a whale-shaped walkie-talkie with a jaw that swung open and shut, a set of earphones, and a hand-stitched case – which read LEND ME YOUR EARS – that clipped onto an adjustable belt. She fastened the belt around her waist and glanced at the user's instruction manual. It was only a couple of pages long, and the print was big enough to read from across a Ping-Pong table.

"You can't imagine how depressing my job gets," said the woman as she checked off Lindsey's name in a superannuated ledger. "When visitors arrive, my hopes always go way up – only to be crushed within minutes. I had to let two boys in the other day, and all they could remember was 'Little Miss Muffet.' It made me want to crawl under the desk and cry."

"I'll get to meet the kids?"

"Take that worried look off your face. You'll be meeting them soon enough," she said kindly. "Things might seem different here at first, but before you know it you'll be settling in nice and easy."

Lindsey welcomed the reassurance. She was full of questions and could use a sympathetic ear. Before she could ask anything, Captain Friedman showed up.

"Make it through immigration?" he asked.

"With flying colors – your young friend just pulled a Shake-speare," beamed the woman. "Here's your visitor's permit, Lindsey."

She gave her a laminated I.D. card, and Lindsey was surprised to see her poem on it.

"Congratulations," said Captain Friedman.

"Is my robot here yet?" asked Lindsey, settling in nice and easy.

"Nope," he said. "We'll just have to get you a dumbot."

"A dumbot?"

"A very low-grade robot, sorry to say. It can't talk. It just toots. One toot means 'No,' two toots means 'Yes.'"

He walked her to the parking lot – no cars anywhere – just bicycles, scooters, dune buggies, go-carts, and rickshaws.

Lindsey heard a roar of engines. A blast of air and she saw two riders on low-flying motor scooters flash overhead, skimming the treetops. An instant later they were gone.

Captain Friedman stared after them in fury. The look on his face was so ferocious that Lindsey's mouth dropped open.

"Stupid kids," he seethed, "itching to get themselves killed."

He angrily snapped his fingers, and a dumbot that looked like a black-and-white-striped camel, or maybe a humpbacked zebra, rounded the corner pulling a rickshaw and knocking the wheels against the curb. Captain Friedman helped Lindsey into the seat and placed her suitcase and travel bag next to her.

"Know your way to Marie Celeste's house? Azure Avenue in the Blue Zone?" he said, and the dumbot tooted three times.

"What does that mean?" asked Lindsey.

"It means this dumbot's a lemon."

He snapped his fingers again. A dumbot that resembled *Mad* magazine's cartoon mascot came running, took its place at the rickshaw, and gave Lindsey an idiotic grin.

"Alfred, can you get to Marie Celeste's?" asked Captain Friedman.

"Toot, toot," went the dumbot.

Lindsey shifted her position to make room for the captain, but he didn't get in.

"So you're all set, Lindsey. Don't forget our bargain."

With a tingle of fear, it dawned on her that he intended to leave her all by herself.

"You aren't coming with me!" she exclaimed, goose bumps racing up and down her arms.

"I'm rollerblading home," he said amiably. "You don't need an escort, do you?"

"How can I find you again?" she said, suddenly feeling both panicky and foolish at the same time.

"Just call my name into your walkie-talkie. It'll automatically switch you onto my wavelength."

Noticing her goose bumps, he said, "Hope you've got a jacket. You're below of the equator now – won't be hot like San Diego."

He snapped his fingers, and the dumbot revved up and toted Lindsey off.

*

The rickshaw pulled up to Number One Azure Avenue, an official-looking residence with a double-decker wraparound porch, flags flying from the roof, and grounds that sprawled like a golf course. A band of tiny robots, which reminded Lindsey of picture-book elves, were busy manicuring the lawn with tweezers. They stopped working and jerked their heads in her direction.

"This is my aunt's house?" she asked, half hoping she'd arrived at the wrong address. She hadn't expected anything so grandiose, and she was already beginning to feel intimidated.

"Toot, toot," went Alfred.

"So, I get out here?"

"Toot, toot."

"Hey, Alfred," she said, dragging her luggage onto the sidewalk. "Want to help me carry my things?"

"Toot!" The dumbot took off snickering to itself.

She hauled her bags along the gravel path and up the stairs to the front door, which was decorated with a wide-brimmed, gold-trimmed, military-style hat with a sash that almost hid the knocker. Finding no bell, she tapped, and the door swung open. A tall, distinguished-looking man in a crisp, blue tuxedo stepped out and took her bags.

"Miss Lindsey? I'm Jeeves," he said. "Do come in. Your aunt is waiting for you."

He led her into an elegant drawing room, an upscale version of the jet. A vaulted ceiling arched like eyebrows over heavily drawn curtains, and mahogany cabinets lined the walls displaying trophies and medallions polished to a deep luster.

Propped on upright chairs by the fireplace were two rail-thin women. The taller one had a pale, oblong face with sharp features. The shorter one had a pale, oblong face with blunt features. Identical cones of blue-gray hair crowned their heads like bee hives balancing on their twig-like necks.

"Miss Lindsey's arrived," announced Jeeves, and the women looked her way.

The tall, sharp-featured woman stood up first. There was a no-nonsense air about her. She was dressed in a well-starched suit, her posture stiff and erect.

Lindsey suddenly became aware of the rumples in her skirt. She hastily smoothed them out, glad that she'd opted against wearing jeans.

"Welcome, my dear. I'm your great aunt, and –" She stopped in mid-sentence and gasped. Whatever she was about to say didn't come out. She stared at her grandniece through bulging eyeballs.

"Oh, my, my, my –" she stammered.

"My, my, my –" stammered the other woman.

"You look just like –"

"Just like –" came the echo.

"Just like your father," Marie Celeste managed to say, but her complexion turned a chalkier shade of pale.

"Guess I do," said Lindsey, wondering what was wrong with the way she looked.

The aunt recovered her composure and held out her bony, jewel-studded fingers for Lindsey to shake. "Let me introduce you to my secretary, Miss Prymm," she said.

"Ummm … pleased to meet you, Miss Prymm," said Lindsey.

Miss Prymm shook hands but didn't respond. She continued to stare at Lindsey.

"You're to call me Aunt Marie Celeste," said the aunt. "Why do you call yourself Lindsey? Your real name is Melinda, isn't it?"

"That was my mother's name. My real name is Rosalind."

Marie Celeste grabbed her stomach as if she'd been punched, and she started hyperventilating. The only sound in the room was her choppy breathing, and Lindsey couldn't think of one thing to say.

Jeeves saved the situation. "Shall I serve the refreshments now?"

"Yes," gasped Marie Celeste. Without removing her eyes from her niece, she gingerly lowered herself into her seat. "No need to be overly formal with a child your age, so I'll call you Lindsey. Now sit down and tell me all about yourself."

Feeling extremely ill-at-ease, Lindsey caught her toe on the edge of a Persian carpet and almost missed the chair before landing in it.

She scowled at her sandal and mumbled, "I'm twelve years old, and I'm going into seventh grade."

"Hmmm. It's never too early to start aging gracefully," observed the aunt. "Do you like to watch television?"

"Sometimes."

"Good. It will give you something useful to do. Young people shouldn't take too much mental or physical exercise. It strains the nervous system."

"Nervous system," said Miss Prymm.

"How is your father?" asked the aunt.

"Fine. He's in Australia. He told me to send you his love."

Marie Celeste acknowledged the sentiment with a nod. "What's he doing there?"

"He's an anthrozoologist..."

"Always was a strange sort of boy. Untidy habits and that sort of thing. So he went off and left you by yourself in California?"

Lindsey bristled. "He isn't strange now. And his ... uh ... his companion was taking care of me. She's the one who talked to you on the phone."

"You must mean his fiancée. I thought it was some sort of high-voltage dumbot the way she kept tooting 'Yes' at me. So he's going to get married again."

"Maybe at the end of the summer when he gets back home."

"I approve of that. Dumbots make reliable wives. They like to stay home and watch television. She'll set a good example for you."

Lindsey decided she did not like her aunt.

Jeeves carried in a silver tray and served boiled ice water into fluted goblets and tapioca pudding into small crystal bowls. He passed the refreshments around and left wordlessly. The aunt tossed down her drink in one neat swallow while the secretary sat stone still, her eyes flitting back and forth between Lindsey and Marie Celeste.

"I suppose you'd like to know why you're here, Lindsey. You'll soon discover that I have a strong sense of duty. You are an O'Neill, after all, and you're at the right age to benefit from my instruction. I see you've earned yourself a walkie-talkie so I shall assume you're trainable."

"Trainable," said Miss Prymm.

"What I'm referring to is proper social etiquette, and I certainly can't trust your father to instill the finer points."

Lindsey took a gulp of water to stop herself from saying anything rude. She couldn't believe how snotty her aunt was, and etiquette or no etiquette she wasn't about to put up with any more jabs at her father.

"For example, and let's call this lesson one," said Marie Celeste, "a young lady should chew as little as possible, otherwise she looks like a cow ruminating on its cud. Whenever you eat, take just a small spoonful and let it slide gracefully over your palate and down your throat. Clear? I, personally, prefer never to chew at all. In order to help you get accustomed to eating like a civilized person, we'll start your regime immediately. Every day your ration of solids will be reduced. Have you finished your pudding?"

"Yes," said Lindsey even though she hadn't taken a single bite.

"In that case, I'll have Jeeves show you up to your room so that you can unpack." Marie Celeste picked up a bronze hammer and struck it against an overhanging gong. "Be sure to stay upstairs and watch television."

"Watch television," said Miss Prymm.

"I have some important visitors coming, and we have serious matters to discuss. You'll soon discover that the political situation here is an ongoing concern, which leaves me very little free time. I doubt I'll see much of you, but I'll give you your assignments each morning at breakfast. I shall expect you to meditate on your etiquette lessons and amuse yourself in a quiet, dignified, ladylike fashion. You may, of course, read your Shakespeare. You'll find a copy on the night table in your room."

Lindsey mustered a weak smile.

"Let me brief you on Paradisian politics," continued the aunt. "We have two opposing parties, the Blues and the Pinks, and there are some uncommitted citizens who call themselves Whites. However, I do not believe in involving children in politics until after they have benefited from a sound education. So go upstairs and don't come down unless I send for you."

"Yes, Aunt Marie."

"Aunt Marie Celeste," she corrected.

"Yes, Aunt Marie Celeste."

"I disapprove of nicknames. Whenever possible, a lady should always refer to people by their full names. That's lesson two."

"Full names," said Miss Prymm. Then she blurted, "But not *yours!*"

Marie Celeste shot her secretary a murderous look. "I'll handle things *my* way," she said.

With a flick of her wrist she dismissed her grandniece from her presence.

Feeling a great deal like Dorothy in *The Wizard of Oz*, Lindsey almost clicked her heels before following Jeeves out. But just before the door shut behind her, she glanced over her shoulder and saw the two hive-headed women nose to nose whispering. So much for proper etiquette.

Chapter Five

BLUE HAVEN

Lindsey unpacked in less than a minute. She slammed her travel bag into a drawer, dumped the contents of her suitcase onto the bed, and pitched her sandals into the closet. She did not feel like behaving.

It looked like the summer was ruined, and Lindsey was so hopping mad that she had to blow off steam. She paced back and forth staring at the carpet and working herself into a sweat.

"My aunt's an old crab," she seethed, "a nasty old control freak. And I'm wearing a *dress!*"

Lindsey tore it off, put on her rattiest T-shirt and jeans, and pulled her hair into two ponytails. When she was satisfied that she looked as unladylike as possible, she began stomping around the room trying to decide what to do. There were no games in sight, not even a deck of cards, and the only book was a fat hardback, *The Complete Works of William Shakespeare.* She felt like throwing it out the window.

Not that Lindsey was prone to tantrums. With Mr. Nice Guy for a father, life usually went her way, and she had little cause to rebel. But lately she'd been running into too much flack to handle by herself, and she'd formed the habit of turning to her mother for guidance.

What would she be doing? Lindsey asked herself. The answer was always the same – she'd be dealing with the problem, not carrying on like a big baby.

Lindsey had read her mother's book on self-empowerment and recalled something in it called "the golden mean," an ancient concept about the balance between head and heart, a kind of link between clear thinking and courage. Lindsey wasn't sure she understood it very well, but the idea had taken hold.

Get a grip on your feelings, she told herself, and start using your brain. Downhearted but dry-eyed, she came to a standstill and tried to get her mind working.

My aunt is pretty high-maintenance, she decided, but at least she doesn't pretend to be nice. Having survived a week with a pain like Tiffany, Lindsey figured she could stand a short stay with a crab. And then what? Australia? She'd have to make sure her father could keep her or she might wind up with Tiffany again, and that was too awful to risk. Anything had to be better than putting up with *her* all summer, and life would have to get a whole lot worse before she'd consider going back.

The only thing to do is try to put up with my aunt, she concluded grimly, until I've worked out a getaway plan.

Once Lindsey had calmed down, she noticed a built-in television at the far end of the room. She was surprised she hadn't seen it before – it spanned the wall like cellophane.

She picked up the remote and idly surfed the channels – nothing but talk shows, reality re-runs, soaps, and political sound bites. Yawn. When she came to Pensioners' Paradise Update (PPU) a breaking news item caught her eye: an ostrich was attempting to cross a busy intersection. Tires screeched, horns honked, dumbots tooted, and traffic came to a roaring standstill as the wild-eyed bird vaulted between vehicles, pecking at shiny objects like door handles, windshield wipers, and headlights.

A police wagon crammed into the fray, and a whiskery-faced officer jumped out shouting and waving his ten-gallon hat. With a hearty squawk, the ostrich attacked the wagon and bit off the rear view mirror, sending the officer into a rage. He swung his billy club and clouted the tail feathers. Startled from behind, the ostrich whipped its head around, snapped off the officer's sunglasses, and gulped down the pieces.

The news program abruptly cut away from the scene to zoom in on City Hall where an announcer introduced Mayor Mandher and his wife. The mayor, a roly-poly black man dressed all in blue from his hat to his spats to his gloves, was delivering a speech on wildlife control.

"I always say, precisely and predictably, duty is a great responsibility," puffed the mayor. "Do your duty! Ban the animals! Make it safe to walk the streets! In tomorrow's elections, vote for leashes and muzzles and ME!" He looked around for applause, and his wife dutifully started clapping.

"Muzzle the mayor," yelled an old woman in a pink beret.

The audience booed and stamped, but Mayor Mandher pretended not to notice. He pushed his face into the camera and smiled from ear to ear, displaying a mouthful of crooked teeth.

"Crooked!" shouted the spectators.

BZZZT, SPUT-SPUT-SPUT, ZONK!

The TV screen fizzled and blanked out. Lindsey flipped the stations. All dead.

A tapping at the door brought her to her feet. "Who's there?" she asked.

"Jeeves."

"Come in."

"Sorry to disturb you, Miss, but you might have noticed the power failure. I thought I'd better warn you before my batteries run out."

"You're a robot!"

"At your service. I'm on reserve-mode, but I can't last for more than a few hours without a recharge."

Jeeves went to the pile of clothes and started folding. Unaccustomed to having servants, Lindsey helped put her things away.

"You look so human," she said.

"Do you think I look like George Washington?" Jeeves gave her a smile that said, "Say yes."

"Well, sort of." The resemblance didn't grab her.

"I'm getting on in years, but I was built when the motto 'personalize' was fashionable. Hollywood designers. If you don't need anything, I'd better go downstairs and conserve my energy."

"Are there any games in the house?" she asked.

"A few. Some of us like to relax that way when we're off duty. I'll see what I can find for you."

Once Jeeves had left, she looked around for something to do and decided to try out her walkie-talkie.

"Hello, Captain Friedman?" The mini-screen lit up, and she saw his face.

"Sam Friedman here. That you, Lindsey?"

"Just testing."

"Everything okay?"

"There's a power failure," she said.

"Another blackout. All over Pensioners' Paradise. Before long all the robots will be crashing."

"How long does it last?"

"No way to tell. Maybe until after the elections."

"Tomorrow?" she asked.

"Yup. We have elections every week. I call them 'The Sunday Night Fights.' Keeps your aunt pretty busy."

"That's why she's making me stay in my room?"

"Probably. She's the Blue Party Chair. She picks the candidates."

"I'd kind of like to go out."

"Enjoy it while you can," he said unconcerned. "You won't be there much longer."

"You've made plans for Australia!"

"Not so fast, little girl. I can't just drop everything from one minute to the next. Call me back in a few days if you're still hankering to leave. You might have a change of heart."

"We made a bargain."

"Not to worry. I won't forget. Sorry, but I've got to ring off. A dumbot just fell into my swimming pool. If its battery is still running, it might electrocute the flying fish. Have a good day."

"Sure, have a good day," she grumbled. "Everything's weird, and I'm stuck in my room, and my aunt's a crab, and … like … what's going on here anyway?"

The J-word popped into her mind, and she wondered how much her dad knew about Pensioners' Paradise. Not much, she suspected, otherwise he'd have prepared her better or maybe refused to let her come. He wouldn't purposely make me miserable, she thought miserably.

Her head was reeling. Too many unexpected things were happening too fast. Bombarded by so many mixed signals, she couldn't make up her mind what was what. A queasy sensation in her stomach told her that she was really on her own – at least for a few more days. She'd just have to hang in the best she could and try to keep out of trouble. Or else she'd never get a puppy.

With nothing better to do, she picked up *The Complete Works of William Shakespeare* and doggedly read the introduction.

*

A brass band was passing the house. Lindsey dropped her book, ran to the window, and peered out. A parade of people, all dressed in blue, were strutting to the tune of "My Blue Heaven." They waved banners that read:

RE-ELECT JERRY MANDHER!
TRUE BLUE – WE LOVE YOU!
WE WANT MERRY JERRY!

A couple broke from the parade and took the long, winding path up to the house. Lindsey recognized the mayor and his wife, glamorous in her bright blue caftan. Miss Prymm darted out to greet them. No sign of battery failure.

So Miss Prymm isn't a robot, thought Lindsey. Nor the mayor. Nor his wife. She wondered how she was supposed to tell the difference between people and robots.

The walkie-talkie began to vibrate. "Lindsey," came the aunt's voice, "come downstairs in two minutes. Punctually."

Lindsey checked herself in the mirror and decided that her outfit was deliciously tacky. With a wicked grin, she noticed an old stain on the neck of her T-shirt. Perfect!

"Right away, Aunt Marie Celeste."

Finding nobody indoors, she stepped out onto the porch. Marie Celeste, Miss Prymm, and the Mandhers were engaged in rapid-fire conversation. Lindsey stood by until they caught sight of her.

"Good grief, Jerry," exclaimed Mrs. Mandher. "She really does look like –"

"Shhh." He wagged a gloved index finger at his wife. "Marie Celeste gratuitously warned you."

Mrs. Mandher clammed up.

"This is my niece," said Marie Celeste. "Lindsey, please curtsy to Dr. and Mrs. Mandher."

Lindsey felt quite foolish but managed a quick dip of the knees. She consoled herself with the thought that none of her friends were witnessing the goodie-goodie routine.

"I have a few errands for you to do downtown. We need candles, and I want them to match this one," said the aunt, handing Lindsey a finely tapered, royal-blue candle. "Go to Edison's and order a crate. Have him put it on my bill and send it over before sundown, and while you're in town, you're not to drink any water. That's lesson number three."

"It might be prudential to, ahem, send the charming young lady to Blooper's," ventured the mayor.

"Thank you for reminding me, Jeremy, but isn't there anything we can do about the lunatic fringe before –" Marie Celeste noticed Lindsey and stopped short. "I think we'd better discuss this in the house. Miss Prymm, we'll need you to take notes."

The three shuffled inside leaving Mrs. Mandher alone with Lindsey.

"You know, you don't have to look like that if you don't want to," began Mrs. Mandher in a stage whisper.

"Look like what, Mrs. Mandher?" Lindsey was beginning to feel like the record-breaking contestant in a freak show. "Is there something wrong with me?"

"Call me Sally. But not when your aunt's around," she winked. "I, myself, didn't always look like this."

"You didn't?"

"I used to look a lot like my husband. As the saying goes, when married couples live together long enough, they start looking alike. It just about destroyed my self-esteem. So I wrote a letter to one of those before-and-after TV shows that do instant makeovers, and I got picked. Backstage they asked me which movie star I wanted to look like, and I said 'Tina Turner,' and I've been like this ever since."

"Wow!"

39

"Maybe we can get you a makeover if Oprah –"

"What's wrong with the way I look?"

Mrs. Mandher hesitated. "You look like a Pink, and Marie Celeste wants you to be a Blue. If you took that pair of ponytails and pulled them into a nice little cone-shaped bun on the top of your head –"

Marie Celeste and Dr. Mandher came out of the house. Miss Prymm tagged along after them scribbling shorthand into a spiral notebook.

"Lindsey," said the aunt, "first you're to go to Edison's Illuminations for the candles, then to Blooper's Pooper-Scooper Outlet. There's an Anti-Ban-Animal League pep rally or protest march or some such nuisance scheduled after lunch tomorrow, and there will be accident-prone pets swarming all over town. I'll expect Mrs. Blooper to deliver my new pooper-scooper before the trouble starts. Kindly tell her that I wish to exchange my old pooper-scooper for the.... What's the name of the latest model, Jeremy?"

"The S.O.S. 3000. By far the finest pooper-scooper on the market. I've officiously ordered six dozen, and I pledge that as your mayor I will clean up every precinct on these islands. I'll make it safe to walk the streets."

"Have Mrs. Blooper send me an S.O.S. 3000," she told Lindsey. "I'll turn in my old model after the animal alert ends."

"While your charming young niece is in town," said Dr. Mandher, "may I suggest that she aid and abet my great grand-nephew. He's handing out Blue ballots and bumper stickers."

Another kid! Lindsey almost jumped for joy. Things might not be too bad if she had a friend.

"How do I know who he is?" she asked.

"He's a worse egghead than Humpty Dumpty."

"Now, Jerry, don't be unkind," admonished his wife. "He doesn't look at all like an egg." She turned to Lindsey. "He's a lovely boy with the sweetest little face. His name is Ryan Mandher. He's eleven years old and about your height. He's dressed in tennis whites, and you'll find him down by City Hall."

"An African-American Humpty Dumpty," grunted Dr. Mandher.

Marie Celeste brushed past the Mandhers and said to Lindsey, "Follow Azure Avenue to Main Street, turn left, and keep walking straight until you get to the end. Edison's and Blooper's will be on your right, along the waterfront. After you've finished your errands, and not before, you may assist Ryan with the electioneering. You'll find City Hall across from Isosceles Square. Clear? I don't want you to get confused or you might end up wandering heaven knows where."

"I'll be all right," said Lindsey.

"Always keep away from funny neighborhoods. That's lesson number four."

Chapter Six

SOMETHING ROTTEN IN ELSINORE

An extravaganza of luxurious homes lined Azure Avenue: mock Medieval castles, Renaissance palaces, Georgian mansions, and Victorian villas, all of them tucked behind tall trees and squashed onto squares of fenced-in land. The uniformly-primped, emerald-green lawns looked like the grassy stuffing lining the bottom of Easter baskets. Lindsey half expected to see pastel-colored eggs and bunnies poking out from under the hedges.

When she came to the crossing between Azure and Main, a myna bird on an overhead branch began flapping its wings.

"Rose pink in the clink," it warbled.

Lindsey cocked her head to catch the look in its eye.

"Rose pink in the clink," it repeated and flew away.

She turned onto Main Street and found herself caught in the bustle of traffic – tons of people, colored signs, and lights under a blue cloud-ruffled sky. A flurry of energetic oldsters whizzed past her, carrying pickets and political posters. As the residential area fanned out into an open-air mall, she read the names over the shops:

BARDS AND NOBLES BOOK STORE

MONTEZUMA'S MIRACLE MINERAL & HAYFLICKS UNLIMITED

ASIMOV'S ROBOT RESTORATION AND RAPID RENOVATION

THE COFFEE TOFFEE TAFFY TAVERN:
featuring low-cal, low-fat, low-carb, high-octane diet peanut butter fudge

QUAYLE'S QWALITY DUMMBOT SHOPP

IMELDA'S SHOE & SUE SHACK:
with bargain basement footwear & legal advice to boot

ZEE ROCK'S REPRODUCTIONS

EARTHA'S EXOTIC ANIMAL EMPORIUM & KIT-KAT CARNIVAL

The last of these was boarded up. A sign hung over the entrance: CLOSED UNTIL FURTHER ELECTIONS.

At the end of Main Street, she came to a tower called Yung Lu's Apolitical Asiatic Gourmet Bistro-Teca, and she paused to read the promo: ONE-HUNDRED-AND-TWO YEARS OF FANCY FOOD FARE. The proprietor himself, a wiry cricket of a man with a five-foot-long white pigtail, was tearing a pink menu off the door and replacing it with a blue one. Yung Lu was the first stationary person she'd come across, and she eyed him with undisguised curiosity.

"Who are you?" he asked.

"Lindsey O'Neill."

"Enough to turn your stomach. I never eat this rubbish myself. Just look at tonight's menu."

BARGAIN BLUE PLATE DELIGHT – $8.88

Purée of Soft Boiled Egg Noodles
Mashed Sweet and Sour Bluefish with Strained Vegetables
Chunkless Chow Mein Sludge
Fortune Cookie Crumbs in Blueberry Syrup Sauce
(Tea and Sympathy Not Included)

When she finished reading, he asked, "You don't want to book a reservation, do you?"

Lindsey shook her head.

"The place will be crawling with Blues tonight. The weekly Night-Before-Victory Benefit Banquet. Just my luck there's a blackout," he said gloomily. "My dumbots crashed, and my electric pulverizer-pounder-processor can't homogenize. Looking for a temporary job?"

"No, thanks, I'm just passing by," said she. "How come everything on the menu is mashed or mushed? Don't people here ever chew anything?"

"Not the Blues. Getting worse ever since that orthodontist got elected."

"Dr. Mandher's an orthodontist?"

"Retired, but he's the one who invented the heavy-metal Brace the Face Special."

An involuntary chill ran down her spine.

"Tell you what," he said, brightening, "you like good Chinese cooking?"

"Sure."

"Come on by at lunchtime tomorrow, and I'll treat you to some royal recipes that I filched from the Manchu Dynasty."

"Manchu?"

"Man chew, girl chew too," he chuckled. "See you tomorrow."

*

Outside City Hall, a baby-faced boy in tennis whites was passing out ballots and bumper stickers. He had a dark tawny complexion, a close-cropped Afro, and a long-suffering attitude, his movements slow and clumsy. When he turned to face her, she was struck by the alert expression in his eyes.

"Are you Ryan?" she asked, only to be polite. One glimpse was enough to dispel any doubts about his identity. "I'm Lindsey. Your uncle sent me to help with the handouts."

Lindsey! The girl with the question mark by her name!

Ryan was so overjoyed to see her that he surprised himself by exclaiming, "All done! Want to go for an ice cream?" And he tossed the stack of handouts into a recycling bin.

Lindsey's empty stomach almost answered for her. "Great, but I've got to do a couple of errands for my aunt."

Ordering candles at Edison's took no time, but Blooper's was a different story. Everybody in town had heard about the animal parade, and a mob scene was gathering along the sidewalk. The rowdy senior citizens hurtled insults as they elbowed each other and crammed through the doorway. A full-scale riot was averted when Mrs. Blooper, a hefty woman with an even heftier voice and the people skills of a walrus, barged out the door threatening her customers with her ham-sized fists.

A pink, white, and blue pushcart labeled "FLEECER'S DEALS ON WHEELS" pulled up to the curb, and a greasy little man in a loud suit and gobs of jewelry started working the crowd.

"Step right up, folks! Step right up! Get your solar-powered generator and beat the blackout!" he hollered.

People came clamoring from all directions. The hoards inside Blooper's crushed back out the door to compete for the generators, and the shop emptied. The defection of her customers did nothing to improve Mrs. Blooper's mood. She stormed back inside and began yanking a sloth-like robot by the tail, trying to attach it to a rusty generator.

Lindsey and Ryan made their way to the counter.

"Hold your horses," she told them. "Just want to see if I can get this hunk of junk working." She pushed a button, and the sloth opened its eyes, smiled, and looked around at everything except the people.

"Talk to the robot," said Mrs. Blooper, waddling away. Her prodigious rump bounced under her skirt like a sack of basketballs.

"I'd like to exchange my aunt's pooper-scooper," said Lindsey.

The sloth fixed its eyes on a spot several inches above her head and asked, "Do ... you ... know ... today's ... exchange ... rate?"

"No," said she.

"Then ... you ... can ... not ... exchange ... it."

Mrs. Blooper waddled back and switched off the generator. The sloth curled itself into a ball.

"I shouldn't waste my energy on it," she scowled. "I keep it around for sentimental reasons. Reminds me of my poor, dear husband – lazy old clunk."

The sloth opened its eyes, sneezed, and closed them again. Mrs. Blooper shoved it under the counter.

"What do you want, girlie?" she asked Lindsey. "An S.O.S. 3000?"

"Yes. For my Aunt Marie Celeste O'Neill. She'll turn in her old one later."

"Tell her I'll send my son Johnny."

"You've got a kid?" asked Lindsey excitedly.

"I'd hardly call him a kid. He's eighty-three years old." Mrs. Blooper retired into the back room yelling, "Johnny!"

Lindsey fell into step with Ryan and headed along Harbor Road toward McSolid's Food Factory.

*

"When did you get here?" asked Ryan, dipping his spoon into a banana split.

"Today." Lindsey contentedly sampled her peach melba parfait. "You like it here?" she asked.

"What do *you* think? You met my uncle."

Ryan wrapped his fingers around his throat and pretended to strangle himself. He was aiming at a comic effect, but Lindsey got the opposite impression.

"That bad?"

"Aunt Sally's all right, I guess. She takes me waterskiing, and she lets me eat solids when old Brace the Face isn't around. She says Unkie used to make her wear a giant tooth costume until she took an assertiveness training course."

"You go waterskiing a lot?" asked Lindsey, hoping to wangle an invitation.

"Just learning." He cast a longing glance at the boats lining the bay.

A party of oldsters entered the snack bar, grumbling about the kids on Elsinore. When they saw Lindsey and Ryan, they pointedly turned around and left.

Ryan's face clouded over. He started to say something but changed his mind, and Lindsey wondered what was bothering him. She idly read the place mat.

"Hey, they've got free computer time here," she said.

"Not much use when the power's down. The batteries die out fast."

"If the oldies have so much high tech stuff, why don't they solve the energy problem?"

"Hard to tell. Nothing normal works here. The minute I landed, my cell phone did a melt down. The electrical force is haywire – messes up all my e-games. You should see what it does to the needle on my compass."

"Topsy-turvy?" she said, picturing the needle twisting into a pretzel.

"The oldies are crazy too. It's like something about this place does things to their brains and drives them cuckoo."

"Could be that water they've got? We'd better not drink it."

"Montezuma water. Named after Montezuma II, the ninth Aztec emperor in Mexico. Aunt Sally says he discovered the Fountain of Youth."

"He did?"

Ryan rolled his eyes.

The conversation stalled out. He slurped, and she munched, and they both pondered the situation.

"You know, Lindsey, there's something weird going on."

"Everything's weird here."

"I mean really weird."

"Like what?" she asked.

"Like did anybody explain to you why all of a sudden out of thin air you were invited to come here?"

"How do you know it was all of a sudden out of thin air?"

"Well, was it?"

"More or less," she said, frowning.

"And you'd never heard of your aunt before you came?"

"Not exactly." Her frown deepened. "How come you know?"

"Every kid I've asked says the same thing. And the day I arrived I met four boys at the airport – four white kids about our age. They looked like cousins or something like that. And here's the worst part – I haven't seen them since. It's like they've disappeared into nowhere."

"How long ago?" she asked.

"Almost a week."

"Maybe they're on one of the other islands?"

"Their baggage tickets said 'Elsinore.'"

47

They locked eyes, both thinking the exact same thing – there were practically no kids on Pensioners' Paradise, but there were hundreds if not thousands of spry, healthy-looking, old people. The oldsters badly outnumbered the kids.

Lindsey broke the silence. "My aunt says she invited me so she can teach me etiquette."

"You're kidding? You believed her?"

"What did they tell you?"

"My uncle says he wants to give me a political education. But I'm positive that's not the real reason. Every time I ask a question he tells me to go watch television. Oldies never give straight answers."

"Could be they need us to run errands and stuff during the blackouts?" she said.

"Just keep your eyes and ears open and pretty soon you're going to notice that something really rotten's going on in Elsinore. And the oldies are all in on it."

"Maybe it's the Pink and Blue business?" The J-word crossed her mind, but she didn't quite dare use it. "Ryan, do I look like a Pink?"

"Are you crazy? Forget the Pinks and the Whites and the Blues," he snapped. "Forget about appearances. That stuff will just confuse you. I'm telling you that all the oldies, and I mean every last one of them, are purposely keeping something from us. And whatever it is, it isn't good."

A long, uncomfortable pause blotted the air between them. Ryan crossed his arms over his chest. Lindsey looked out the window and saw a really good-looking boy with an athletic build and a glorious suntan, strolling hand in hand with a girl who had masses of blond hair. Lindsey would have traded a year's allowance for hair like that. She watched until they passed out of sight.

"You know them?" she asked.

"I've seen them around."

"She's only twelve years old?"

"Almost thirteen."

Lindsey found herself hoping the blonde would turn thirteen so fast that she'd be deported before anyone had time to sing "Happy Birthday."

"Ken and Barbie," said Ryan. "Just arrived and they're already an item."

"That's their real names?"

"His name is Zach. Hers is C-E-R-I-S-E pronounced 'Sir Ease' or something like that."

"Maybe they can tell us what's going on."

He shrugged. "Might as well ask a dumbot."

"So what are we going to do?"

"Start investigating – the faster the better. Think about it, Lindsey, we're trapped. Let's say we want to get out of here, how are we going to do it?"

She didn't like that idea one bit, and she wondered how far she could trust Captain Friedman. He was probably just as soft in the head as the other oldies.

"I'll call my dad," she said.

"He knows how to find you here?"

"I ... uh ... I guess...." Her voice faded out as her mind started racing. "It's got to be on a map."

"Want to bet? I checked an atlas before I came, and Pensioners' Paradise wasn't in it. And it's nowhere on the net. So I called a travel agency, and they'd never heard of it. I'm not sure where we are even though I tried to gauge it from the direction the plane was heading."

"So why did you come?"

"My mother made me. She wanted to get rid of me for the summer. How about you?"

"Nobody exactly forced me," she said, before recalling how gleefully Tiffany had sped her to the airport.

"I bet nobody made plans for getting you back home either."

"You don't think they want to keep us here forever?" She paused to reflect, and her imagination conjured up spine-tingling scenarios.

"Dunno," said Ryan. "But we'd better find out."

*

Darkening shadows stretched the mask of night. Sidewalks emptied, buildings dimmed, and only the random candle flickered behind window shades. Lindsey quickened her pace as she wound her way back to her aunt's house. Pensioners' Paradise was beginning to look like a nightmare, and she wished she hadn't come.

When she got to the corner of Azure and Main, she took a quick glance at the spot where she'd seen the myna bird. In its place, a hoot-owl loomed over her like a threat. An icicle of terror cut through her. She screamed into her walkie-talkie. "Ryan! Ryan!" No answer. "Captain Friedman!"

"Nobody is here to take your call. If you want to view my home page, press one. If you want to hear my latest hit tune, press two. If you want –"

Something rustled in the shadows. Spooked out of her mind, Lindsey rounded Azure Avenue and ran home faster than she'd ever run before. She burst through the door, charged up the stairs, and nosedived into bed.

Chapter Seven

OF BARDS AND BONDS

When Lindsey slunk into the dining room the next morning, Jeeves was serving Sunday brunch to the aunt, the mayor, and the secretary.

"Good morning, everybody," she said, making an effort to sound cheerful. No point letting them know how she really felt.

The adults barely nodded, and she took a seat as far away from them as possible. She hoped they'd forget she was there so that she could observe their behavior. Maybe she could pick up a couple of clues.

With growing curiosity, she noticed that Mayor Mandher wore gloves even during meals. Another odd thing about him was the bruise mark just below his hair line. She was positive that it hadn't been there yesterday, but nobody at the table said anything about it. Nor did they mention the way Miss Prymm kept patting her hair-hive with her napkin.

"The power's back so we're off to an early start," said Marie Celeste. "There's plenty of work to do before this evening's elections."

Lindsey poured herself some juice. Before she could stop it, Jeeves ladled runny porridge into her bowl.

"You're not chewing, are you?" scolded Marie Celeste.

The aunt, the mayor, and the secretary turned their heads in unison and stared while Lindsey took a tiny spoonful of porridge, slipped it onto her tongue, and let it slide gracefully over her palate and down her throat. The three oldies kept their eyes on her as she repeated the performance. By the third spoonful, they tired of watching and turned their attention to their own food.

"As soon as you finish breakfast, you can go to your room and watch television all day," said the aunt. "The Anti-Ban-Animal League marchers will be blocking the downtown area, and the Pinks are apt to cause problems, so you're better off at home. I'll have Jeeves blend you your TV meals."

Lindsey bit her lip self-consciously. "Like ... uh...."

"If you have anything to say, kindly do so," said Marie Celeste.

"I'm invited to Yung Lu's for lunch."

"Probably leftovers from last night's pre-victory banquet. I hear it was a flop." Marie Celeste raised an eyebrow. "He forgot to put the fortunes into the cookie crumbs, and the mashed bluefish was tough."

"Tough," said Miss Prymm.

"I'll call Yung Lu and cancel," smiled the aunt.

"Let's not be overly hasty, Marie Celeste," said the mayor. "Appearances might not be so apparent. We can't be too sure which ticket Yung Lu is backing in the elections."

Marie Celeste raised both eyebrows. "What do you mean, Jeremy? Can't we count on his vote anymore?"

"Not after last night's brawl, I'm afraid. Some of our finest citizens, some of our *very* finest citizens, politely vociferated our freeedom of speech, and Yung Lu grew violent. Constables had to break it up."

"Hmmm. Then maybe she'd better go. Every vote counts, and it might offend him if she cancels last minute." Marie Celeste nodded as if agreeing with herself and addressed her niece. "I certainly don't envy you. The food is appalling, but be sure to tell Yung Lu how delicious his leftovers are. It's never wise to offend a prospective voter. That's lesson number five."

"May I be excused from the table?" asked Lindsey. "Please."

"Certainly, my dear, as soon as you've voted for the mayor." Marie Celeste passed her a Blue ballot and a pen. "Your signature is to be placed clearly on the dotted line."

"I'm not old enough to vote. And you told me you didn't think kids should be involved in politics."

"Charming young lady," said Dr. Mandher with a sour expression on his face.

"Stuff and nonsense, Lindsey, you're not involved. This is an *absentee* ballot," said the aunt. "And furthermore, we permit no age discrimination on Pensioners' Paradise."

Lindsey signed the ballot and handed it back. "Can I go now? I'd like to phone Ryan."

"He's out on the porch –" began Dr. Mandher.

"You mean the verandah," said Marie Celeste.

"Ah, yes, the verandah. I distinctively instructed him to stay there. The little ingrate is probably reading something behind my back," said Dr. Mandher. "It better not be a history book."

"Good heavens, Jeremy, you don't let that boy read history, do you?"

"Of course not, but he's the sneaky type."

Marie Celeste grew stern. "You mustn't read history, Lindsey. It's very bad for you. A wise and prophetic philosopher named Jorge Santayana claims that people who don't read history get to relive it. Keep that in mind if you ever feel tempted."

"That doesn't make any sense," said Lindsey. "I mean, like the people who read it and the people who don't read it aren't exactly on different planets. So how can some be reliving history when others aren't?"

"Never question the notions of great philosophers, my dear. They're paid to think for us, and we deserve to get our money's worth. Let me assure you that I, personally, took Mr. Santayana's words to heart and stopped reading history entirely. Having liberated my mind from the constricting influence of facts, I have enabled myself to resurrect the glorious world of the past. Every year at the Elsinore Shakespeare Festival, I become a time-traveler, a perfect human anachronism. Tell her, Miss Prymm, am I a perfect anachronism?"

"Yes, indeed," said Miss Prymm, looking quite pleased with herself.

Just for the sake of needling her aunt, Lindsey said, "The book in my room says that Shakespeare wrote histories."

"He never stooped to history! His historical plays are Art!" Marie Celeste looked so cross that Lindsey immediately flipped into best behavior.

"I'm sorry, Aunt Marie Celeste," she said, uncertain why she was apologizing, but it seemed to be expected.

"Why don't you take Ryan into the den to watch TV," said the aunt. "I'm certain he'd rather do that than read. And be sure to offer him some freshly boiled ice-water."

"I'll go see." Lindsey sprang to her feet and rushed out before her aunt could deliver another etiquette lesson.

*

"What are you reading?" asked Lindsey. It looked like an encyclopedia.

Ryan flicked his eyes from the page. "Geology."

"Yucksville."

"It might save our lives."

"Come off it."

It struck her that Ryan was a bit of a worry wart. He'd gotten her so rattled that she'd let herself be frightened by a hoot-owl.

"When you were flying in, did you notice anything strange about the land mass formations of these islands?" he asked.

"They sort of looked like prehistoric anthills."

"Brilliant observation." He made a goofy face that annoyed her.

"If you're so smart, what was I supposed to notice?"

"A mammoth volcano."

"Duh! Of course I saw it." It was her turn to make a goofy face.

"It's an anomaly," said Ryan.

"What?"

"Abnormal. It says right here that there isn't any volcanic activity in this part of the South Pacific."

"Ryan, does the book say anything about … uh … a Jedgar?"

"A Jedgar?"

"Shhh! Just look it up."

She peered over his shoulder as he flipped through the index and found nothing. Then he checked the glossary. Nothing.

"What's a Jedgar supposed to be?"

"That's what I'd like to know." She hesitated before posing

her next question. "Can I trust you to keep a secret? If you tell anyone, I might get into trouble."

The lawn elves stopped tweezing the grass, rotated their heads, and blinked. The tiny antennas on their foreheads bent like periscopes and started vibrating.

"I've got a feeling we're already in trouble" said Ryan.

Lindsey whispered into his ear her conversation with Captain Friedman about the Jedgar.

"Interesting," said Ryan. "Maybe we can find out about it at the Elsinore Public Library. My aunt's the librarian. She might let us see the books if –"

"We need permission?"

"Uh-huh. There's a big sign over the main desk. It says: NEITHER A BORROWER NOR A LENDER BE."

"You're serious? How are we supposed to find out anything?"

"Internet."

"Or maybe that book store — Bards and Nobles?"

"I've already been there. All they've got is poetry," said he.

"Hey, that reminds me, you didn't answer last night when I called you on my walkie-talkie."

"I don't have one."

"Can't you buy one?"

He shook his head. "The only way to get one is to recite Shakespeare."

"You don't know any at all?"

"No."

"How did you get through immigration?" she said sarcastically, "'Little Miss Muffet?'"

"I recited 'Paul Revere's Ride.'"

"No way! That's the longest poem I've ever seen."

"I felt like showing off that day. I've got a photographic memory. The immigration lady nearly kissed me, but she wouldn't give me a walkie-talkie."

"If you've got a photographic memory, you'd better learn some Shakespeare and get yourself a walkie-talkie fast. I mean, what if we need to call each other?"

She dashed upstairs and came back with *The Complete Works of William Shakespeare*.

"Can you find a poem with animals in it?" he asked skeptically. "That might not be too terrible. I'm not memorizing any sappy love poems."

"Here," she said, pointing out a selection.

"That's Shakespeare? It looks like a recipe – cooking class at Hogwarts."

"It's a witch's potion from *Macbeth*."

Ryan ran his eyes over it once and handed the book back to her. "Done."

"You already know it by heart?"

"Word for word."

"I don't believe you."

"So, here goes." He took a deep breath and, treating the whole thing as if it were one long sentence, launched into a toneless recital:

> Double, double, toil and trouble,
> Fire burn, and cauldron bubble.
> Fillet of a fenny snake,
> In the cauldron boil and bake.
> Eye of newt and toe of frog,
> Wool of bat and tongue of dog,
> Adder's fork and blind-worm's sting,
> Lizard's leg and owlet's wing,
> For a charm of powerful trouble,
> Like a hell-broth boil and bubble …

"That's awesome!" she exclaimed. They grinned at each other appreciatively.

The aunt, the mayor, and the secretary marched out the door.

"You're missing the *Good Morning Elsinore show*," said the aunt. "What are you children doing out here?"

"Nothing," said Lindsey.

The aunt nodded approvingly. "We're going over to City Hall and won't be back until tonight." She plucked the hat from the door peg, planted it on her head, and tied the sash firmly under her chin.

"You can watch us live on PPU," said the mayor, puffing out his chest.

"PPU," said the secretary.

The three oldies hurried down the path to flag down a rickshaw and tuk-tuk-tuk themselves into town.

"I'm going to the airport to get my walkie-talkie. Wanna come?" asked Ryan.

"No, thanks, I think I'll go to the beach."

"See you later," he said, hopping onto his bike.

"Ryan, don't you wonder what the Jedgar is?"

"Sure, but mostly I wonder what it can do."

"What it can do?"

"To us."

*

The air was sultry and the sun blazed across a cloudless sky. Lindsey took a long swim in the ocean. Then she stretched her limbs, glided over the rushing surf, and floated back to shore. Relaxed and dripping, she shed her worries and waded along the water's edge. Every so often, she passed an oldie or two in a blue bathing suit, on a blue beach towel, under a blue umbrella. She saw no Pinks at all. Maybe they were all in town getting psyched for the Anti-Ban-Animal League march.

Lindsey loved logic, so she decided to puzzle things out step by step. If there was an Anti-Ban-Animal League, it made sense there had to be some sort of ban-animal movement too, and from the look of things it was organized by the Blues. After all, she hadn't seen one live animal since she'd gotten to Elsinore, that is, unless she counted the myna bird and the owl – and that ostrich on TV. She wasn't even sure if Captain Friedman's flying fish were still alive.

But, she reasoned, there had to be animals somewhere on these islands. Blooper's pooper-scooper business was booming. And the oldies had said something about the Pinks bringing their pets into town and creating trouble. She imagined a parade of cats and dogs and heaven knows what types of animals marching along Main Street. It occurred to her that downtown Elsinore might turn into a pretty interesting spot.

Maybe even those four missing kids would show up –
"Hey, there!" A voice broke into her daydreaming. Two sun-baked boys in Hawaiian swimming trunks and backwards base-ball caps were jogging toward her. The older boy took off his cap and waved it at her. He was the Ken-doll dreamboat she'd seen through the snack bar window. The Barbie-doll girlfriend was nowhere in sight.

Maybe she's already been deported, thought Lindsey with a growing sense of well-being.

"You new in town?" The dreamboat flashed her a Chicklet-white grin. "My name is Zachary. Call me Zach."

"I'm Rosalind," she said, blushing, "but my nickname is Lindsey."

"Rosalind. Nice name. I like it." He pressed her hand.

Her blush was spreading fast. She looked down at her toes to see if it had arrived there yet.

"Lover Boy's at it again," sneered the smaller boy.

He was a scrawny kid with a cocksure air and a big mouth. His ears bent inward like a pair of parentheses trying to catch a phrase, and the braces on his teeth reminded her of barbed wire.

"What's your name?" she asked.

"J. Ackerman Bond, but the school computer got it wrong and ran it together, so the teachers all started calling me Jackerman and it stuck."

"They call him *the* Jackerman 'cuz he ain't human."

"He's a robot?" Lindsey took a closer look.

"Nah, he's my little squirt brother. Just call him Jack."

"Zach and Jack. That's kind of cute," said she. "Like a rhyme –"

"Where you staying?" asked Zach, moving in closer.

"With my Great Aunt Marie Celeste at the end of Azure Avenue. How about you?"

"With our great-great grandparents. Boy, are they mental – scared of everything," said Jack, edging in. He pulled a slug from his pocket and let it wriggle under her nose.

"Yuck," went Lindsey.

"These things are worth money. The oldies pay me not to put 'em around the house."

"Bet you haven't seen the place. Big brick building, looks like a fortress." said Zach. "Right by Arden Forest. I can show you around."

"You know what's going on here?" she asked. "Like the volcano and the poems and all the oldie stuff?"

"Been talking to that egghead kid, the mayor's nephew?" he laughed. "Stick with me and you'll have lots more fun."

"Lover Boy's lots of fun – he likes to take long walks in the woods," said Jack.

At loss for what to say, Lindsey suddenly felt like cutting out. She started thinking that if it wasn't too late, she could stop by McSolid's Food Factory and e-mail her father before dropping in at Yung Lu's.

"What time is it anyway?" she asked.

"Eleven o'clock. Whaddya think of my iiiWatch? It's a genuine Electronic Epsilon Delux. I'm gonna be a secret agent when I grow up," said Jack. He flashed the iiiWatch at her. It had more buttons, dials, and knobs than an S.O.S. 3000.

"Eleven o'clock, and it's time to rock," chimed the watch, sparking off a shower of psychedelic lights.

"Where'd you get it?" she asked, duly impressed.

"That's for me to know and for you to find out."

"Wanna go to lunch with me at Maxi's?" smiled Zach. "We can catch the zoo parade in town."

"Not today," she smiled back.

Her answer wiped his smile right off. The look on his face was more shocked than disappointed.

"What about tomorrow?"

"I don't *think* so," she said sweetly. "See you around." She turned on her heel and left.

For the life of her, Lindsey couldn't figure out why she hadn't said "Yes" to a really cute boy she was dying to go out with. Could it have anything to do with that feminine mystique business that Tiffany kept talking about? Was there really any such thing? If so, maybe through pure instinct that airhead Tiffany had latched onto something worth knowing. She always claimed that men liked to be kept waiting. Lindsey muddled it over in her mind and came to no satisfactory conclusion, but the hint of a smile graced her lips. Mysteriously.

Chapter Eight

ECOLOGICAL IMBALANCES

Yung Lu's Apolitical Asiatic Gourmet Bistro-Teca was the tallest edifice in town. It was, in fact, a lighthouse tower that he'd converted into a restaurant. With a touch of whimsy, he'd re-roofed it and affixed a bell-curved, red-tiled, pagoda-style awning, bordered by a brass menagerie of dragon-faced gargoyles. The mayor's architectural-engineering-steering committee had awarded it a runner-up medal in the Seven Wonders of Elsinore contest.

When Lindsey showed up to lunch, Yung Lu was in a frisky mood. He pranced around the kitchen singing:

> *Whistle while you wok*
> *Ta-ta TAH ta-ta-ta TAH...*

"I'm so tickled you're here," he said as he added flourishes to a platter of *mu-gu-gai-pan garni*. "I've got a yen for Far-East food."

With a hearty laugh, he looped his arm through hers and led her to the spiral staircase.

"It's time for a little social climbing." He snapped his fingers, and a dumbot skipped out of the pantry. "Table for two on the roof garden. Take the trays upstairs," ordered Yung Lu, "and don't forget the chafing dishes."

They climbed and climbed and climbed the staircase to the top of the lighthouse and sat down to a genuine feast. Yung Lu pressed a button, and the tower began to revolve like a merry-go-round. He whipped the lids off the platters, and the air mellowed with mouth-watering aromas – ginger and clove and mandarin rind. She popped a glazed water chestnut into her mouth and sighed as it exploded into flavor. They dug into the tangy, bite-sized morsels, each dish more scrumptious than the last, and it struck her as odd that no customers were showing up.

"This is like fabulous," she said, thinking that her friends would flip if they knew she was having a date with a hundred-and-two-year-old man, or maybe his restaurant was a hundred-and-two-years old. In either case, she was having a good time.

"Aw, shucks," he said, twirling his pigtail to disguise his glee. "Get your good days, get your bad days. Today, good day – you're my honored guest. Yesterday, bad day – my place got busted. Blue Plate Delight fight. But who cares? Ho-ho-har-har. I'm insured. Did you catch my picture in today's papers? It's on the front page of The Elsinore X-Press."

"I saw the headlines."

"The headlines! Hahahaha-hee-hee-hee!" He couldn't stop laughing, and Lindsey couldn't figure out what was so funny.

He finally calmed down enough to ask, "Did you happen to see – hahaha – the mayor this morning?"

"Yes."

"Did you – hahaha – notice his *head* line?"

"You mean the bruise mark?"

"The paparazzi snapped my picture when I was clouting him with a mega-mouth chopstick!" Yung Lu grabbed his belly and doubled over into gales of laughter.

"You didn't!"

"I did! During the bluefish brawl. He was at the head table giving me headaches, and when he threatened to shut down my restaurant, I couldn't resist." Yung Lu laughed some more. "Proudest moment of my catering career. I haven't had so much fun since the Boxer Rebellion."

He passed her the newspaper. "I'll make you a copy. Every paper in town was sold out before breakfast."

"I'll frame it and keep it forever," said Lindsey, her dimples positively radiant. "Can't wait to show it to my friend Ryan. He's going to love it."

"Then I'll make two copies. What about a picture of – ha-ha – Miss Prymm, the secretary bird with the nest on her head? There's a good shot of me topping her tangles with blueberry syrup."

Lindsey suppressed a giggle. "Her hair-hive? You poured syrup into –"

"Bingo! She asked for a special order of bird's nest soup, so I gave it to her. Pity your aunt didn't attend," he added wistfully, "my *crowning* moment."

The dumbot cleared the empty bowls and brought up the dessert — caramelized pineapple crunch flambé. When Lindsey sampled it, she almost moaned in ecstasy as it melted in her mouth.

"This is the life," she murmured, savoring the sweetness.

Suddenly the whole tower trembled, and the table overturned, chucking the pineapple platter into Yung Lu's lap.

"Drat that Jedgar!" he cried, forgetting himself before his honored guest. He jumped to his feet, raced to the guardrail, and looked out to sea. Lindsey followed suit.

Hunching over the horizon, the brooding black volcano pursed its lips and spat angry tongues of fire.

"Drat that – Drat that – Drat that Jedgar!" shrieked Yung Lu, beside himself with rage. Like an acrobat, he leaped onto the rail and swung his fists at the volcano.

A sonic-splitting boom shook the tower making it rock back and forth like a toddler's tippy cup. Yung Lu lost his footing, toppled from the rail onto the award-winning roof, and slid downward. He desperately tried to claw his way back up, but the pineapple sauce on his smock acted like an oil slick against the glossy, varnished patina of the tiles.

"Don't look down!" shouted Lindsey. The height and sharp angle of the drop made her dizzy.

Yung Lu painstakingly scratched half way up the rooftop, lost his grip, and slid back down. His fingernails carved ten parallel lines into the shiny red enamel before letting go. Flailing his arms wildly, he cart-wheeled to the outer edge and caught the seat of his pants on the tusks of a brass gargoyle.

"AGHHHHHH!" he yowled, disentangling himself. He

yanked so hard that his pants split at the seams, and Lindsey couldn't help noticing that his underwear was fire-engine red.

"Don't panic!" she cried.

From beneath sparse eyebrows he gave her a withering glance.

"Take it slowly," she begged. "When you get to the top, toss me your pigtail. I'll try to reel you in."

Yung Lu nodded. He inched his way toward her, took aim, and pitched the five-foot-long pigtail in her direction. It flew over the rail, and she snagged it on her first attempt. Worn out and panting, he collapsed onto the ledge.

"You all right?"

He was too winded to answer. She tugged with all her might but couldn't budge him. As the roof garden kept turning around and around, the pigtail chafed her palms. She couldn't hold on much longer.

"Get the dumbot," he wheezed.

"Dumbot! Dumbot!"

"Its name is Fujiyama."

"Fujiyama! Fujiyama!" she called.

"Got to snap your fingers to get 'em to obey."

With both hands clutching onto a pigtail, it wasn't easy to snap her fingers, but she finally managed, and Fujiyama scurried up the stairs. Between them, they dragged Yung Lu to safety and laid him flat on a mat beneath a bamboo umbrella.

"Water" was the last word he uttered before passing out.

Lindsey snapped her fingers, and Fujiyama fetched a pint-sized bottle of Montezuma's Miracle Mineral Shock-Block Formula 57. Using the eye-dropper on the inside of the bottle cap, she administered the dosage indicated on the label until Yung Lu's eyelids fluttered open. His eyeballs rolled around independently of each other like two wonton in a bowl of broth.

"More," he whispered, smacking his lips, and she continued the salubrious drippings until he fully revived.

"Jedgar's Inferno," he said in a small voice. His chest pounded noisily for a moment or two. Then he perked up, propped himself onto his elbow, snatched the bottle, and gulped it down to the very last drop.

"Ahhh." He wiped his mouth with the back of his hand and hopped to his feet, "I'll just have to rename my restaurant the Eiffel Tower."

She looked at him askance. Had the water somehow dampened his wits?

"Don't you get it?" he said brightly. "The *I Fell* Tower!"

Lindsey groaned.

Mount Cinderella was still rumbling. It heaved and panted and belched out smoke like a dragon with its nose on fire. All at once, it contracted, released the pent up pressure, and spat a giant fireball from its cavernous mouth. The fireball shot upward piercing the clouds. When it reached the apex of its parabolic ascent, it hovered for a split second, rotated on its axis, and thundered back down.

Yung Lu and Lindsey watched horror-stricken as it crashed to earth and smashed through the ocean floor. The impact displaced so much water that the entire bay seemed to be draining into an invisible suction cup. Churning like a maelstrom, the water gurgled, bubbled, burped back up, and rushed forth with such force that it set off tidal waves which roared straight into Elsinore.

*

The eruption started and ended so fast that it caught the Anti-Ban-Animal League marchers off guard. Pockets of air carried their frantic wails. All the oldies in town, irrespective of their political biases, were thrown into a state of despair.

Lindsey and Yung Lu ran to the opposite side of the roof to see what was going on downtown. Knee-deep flooding swept over Main Street. Panicky animals broke away from their masters and bolted. A herd of moose got loose, galloped into Arden Forest, and attacked the dogwood trees. Crocodiles snapped their displeasure and slithered along gutters in search of a freshwater habitat. Snorting wallabies stampeded down Azure Avenue at breakneck speed. They scaled the "No Trespassing" signs at a single bound, trampled the landscape gardening, and redecorated it with droppings. And a frantic flamingo, wildly chopping the air, flew up to the dome of McSolid's Food Factory and laid an egg in the satellite dish.

Yung Lu surveyed his garden. "There's a buffalo in my lychee-fruit patch," he bleated, and he raced down the stairs three at a time to alert the kitchen help.

*

By late afternoon, the water had receded. A squadron of robots combed the island for stray pets, and a detachment of dumbots cleared the wreckage. Sirens, bells, horns, whistles, and alarms shrilled from all directions.

Police Chief Constable Dogberry hastily deputized the able-bodied citizens and placed them on round-the-clock duty. Declaring a state of supranational emergency, he commandeered the communications lines and bombarded the airwaves with beastly broadcasts.

Mayor Mandher interrupted the transmission. "Owing to unexplicated changes in the environmental conditions," he announced gravely, "I hereby postpone this evening's elections and declare a state of Mayor-Shall-Rule, which means that nobody is allowed to go anywhere or do anything without my permissiveness."

On the steps of City Hall, Pink Cross relief volunteers set up a collapsible table and dispensed hot cocoa and donuts. Next to them, Fleecer was piling up record-breaking earnings peddling lassoes, traps, cages, muzzles, leashes, nets, and air-guns.

"All unauthorized pedestrians will clear the traffic arteries, walkways, and public areas immediately," barked Dogberry over the wires.

Fleecer and the Pink Cross volunteers reluctantly packed up and dispersed.

*

Yung Lu and Lindsey listened to an oldies-but-goodies station on his monstrous sound system short-wave radio as they dined on the roof garden under the amber glow of rice-paper lanterns. He flipped the dial to catch his favorite program, the *Dim Sum Hit Parade*. When Lindsey tried to get him to talk about Jedgar's Inferno, he said, "Shhh" and turned up the volume. He briskly drummed his chop sticks along to the beat.

"Chip-chop to the hip-hop," he sang at the top of his lungs.

Chief Constable Dogberry cut into the broadcast.

"There's bad news and there's good news," growled Dogberry. "The bad news is that most of the lost animals are still at large, so Mayor-Shall-Rule restrictions will remain in effect until further notice. The good news is that the use of walkie-talkies will be permitted for the next four and a half minutes."

"I'd better phone my aunt and tell her that I can't go home," said Lindsey.

"You're not going home?" The won ton nearly popped out of Yung Lu's eye-sockets.

"How am I supposed to get there? We're not allowed out on the streets."

"We'll call Juanita Shringapur down at the airport. One of her girls can pick you up in a helicopter and drop you off at your aunt's jolly old verandah, ho-ho-ho."

He placed the call. Within minutes, an ultra-modern clipper-copter landed on the roof garden, and an old woman in a jogging suit spirited her aboard. Yung Lu waved good-bye as Lindsey was airlifted over the postcard pretty panorama to be daintily dropped onto the wraparound verandah of Marie Celeste's powder blue mansion.

*

That night Lindsey tossed and turned in bed. Moonshine's watery beams bathed the room in an eerie light, and every time she rolled over, she saw narrow eyes gleaming at her through the window. She yanked the curtains shut and fell into fitful sleep. In the morning, she shrugged it off as a bad dream and forgot about it.

Chapter Nine

CREEPS IN THIS PETTY PACE

Day after day the disaster dragged on. The buffalo roamed and the deer and the antelope played, but the kids in Elsinore were grounded and turning into couch potatoes. Mashed.

Along Azure Avenue, the decibel levels grew unbearable as dumbots set off dynamite to smoke out the lost pets, and a fracas of S.O.S. 3000s clattered over the cobblestones, gobbling pyramids of plops. Overhead the sky hummed with low-flying aircraft, their holds bulging with airborne animals.

Marie Celeste and Mayor Mandher, too distressed to leave the safety of their homes, relayed sensitive documents by shuttle bird service, a fleet of digital pigeons good for carrying lightweight parcels. For reasons deemed highly suspicious, both their properties had turned into breeding grounds for creepers and crawlers. Despite all efforts to clear the neighborhood, stray animals still fed on the garden foliage and made surprise forays through open windows in search of heartier snacks. Unable to adjust to the soft food served, they yowled plaintively at meal times.

Lindsey took in the scene from her window. Below her, platoons of robots equipped with prodders and pitchforks were hacking through the shrubbery to rout out a nest of iguanas. She opened the window and felt a gust of fresh air – a reminder of how badly she wanted to go outdoors.

"Where are you taking the animals?" she shouted.

"None of your busybody business," grunted Assistant Constable Dull from his catcher-copter. He turned back to supervise the safari. "Hurry it up, boys."

"It's time for lesson number six," said the aunt, sashaying into Lindsey's room. "Never scream out an open window unless the house is on fire."

"Aunt Marie Celeste," said Lindsey, "what's going to happen to the animals?"

"They'll be returned to the Pink Zone, but it's nothing to concern you. This time we're going to make sure they stay there. Stiffer leash laws."

"The Pink Zone?" asked Lindsey.

"A funny neighborhood best avoided. You haven't already forgotten lesson number four?" Her eyebrows arched into her head-hive.

"Always keep away from funny neighborhoods."

The answer seemed to reassure Marie Celeste. "Why have you turned off the television, Lindsey?"

"I got tired of it."

"Poor child, you've overexerted yourself. You must keep up your strength. I'll have Jeeves bring you some consommé."

She stepped back to inspect Lindsey. As if attempting to sharpen her focus, her eyebrows crept like steel gray caterpillars toward the bridge of her nose.

"Your clothes! Whatever happened to that sweet little dress you arrived in?"

Before Lindsey could answer, the aunt swept over to the closet and found the sundress.

"Only one dress in your entire wardrobe! And it's soiled! You have nothing decent to wear in society, and you cannot show up at a Blue Party gala looking like a ragamuffin — everybody in Elsinore will be watching you on PPU! Your father will hear about this! I have a thing or two to tell him!"

Lindsey's heart sank as her thoughts flew to her puppy.

"That wretched fiancée of his," seethed the aunt. "I told her that you had to dress like a Paradisian and needed suitable clothes for formal events like inaugural balls! I gave her explicit instructions what to pack!"

Lindsey's mouth dropped open.

"Don't you DARE defend that dreadful woman," said the aunt. "She's unfit for mothering. And the sooner your father knows about it the better." Marie Celeste folded the sundress over her arm. "I'll have this dry cleaned and sent to my tailor. He can use it as a model to start cutting a dress pattern. Wedgwood blue silk should suit your complexion. You'll need fittings…. But first I'm calling your father. He'll have no blessing from me if he marries that woman!"

Having stumbled across an unexpected ally, Lindsey didn't dare jinx her good fortune by grinning, but "bye-bye Tiffany" flashed across her mind.

"How much longer will I be grounded?" she asked.

"Until the animal emergency ends. A mad tiglon is still at large – the biggest feline in Paradise." Marie Celeste shuddered at the thought. "That tiglon beast could *chew* you to ribbons, so kindly don't provoke me with any more impertinent questions."

Lindsey wasn't about to be put off that easily. "Aren't we in danger from the volcano?"

"What volcano? There is no volcano anywhere near here. I'm afraid you have an overly fanciful imagination."

"The volcano on Jedgar's Inferno," whispered Lindsey as she pictured Captain Friedman tearing up her air ticket to Australia.

The aunt clutched her stomach. Her voice climbed to a shriek. "I'll not have you using that kind of language! Where did you hear that wretched word?"

"Somebody must have said it."

"I did not invite you here to pick up foul language. Do not use that word again!"

"I'm sorry, Aunt Marie Celeste," said Lindsey, thoroughly cowed. But she'd heard enough foul language at school to be pretty sure that "Jedgar" wasn't a swear word, and she wondered why it drove the oldies so crazy.

"Furthermore," said Marie Celeste, "we Paradisians do not consider it polite to discuss any kind of inferno."

"But the volcano –"

"I told you quite clearly, there *is* no volcano. Never contradict the leader of a political party. That's number seven."

Marie Celeste switched on the TV and marched downstairs to check the kitchen. Lindsey dropped onto a chaise lounge and watched as an army of dancing bottles came onto the screen, flipping their lids and singing, "Montezuma's Mineral is yummy, yummy, yummy."

Lindsey sang along mechanically. Even though she hated the ad, she'd found herself singing it all week. Try as she might, it was impossible to shake it from her head.

That stupid song is like mind control – it sticks like glue, she thought moodily.

The PPU *News Bulletin* came on.

"The following program is being brought to you by Fleecer's Ballot Shredding Syndicate," said the announcer. "Today's top news stories:

Poochie Blooper dumps the Blues and turns Pink;
Ban on walkie-talkies extended for another twenty-four hours;
Mad tiglon still on the rampage;
McSolid's Food Factory donates four dozen flamingo eggs to the Pink Cross Relief fund.

And here's our roving reporter Squeaky Zeitung bringing you the latest scoop on party poopers – and a hot flash from Candidate Blooper."

BEEP, BEEP, BEEP, BEEP, went the TV, and a mousy little reporter came onto the screen.

"This is Squeaky Zeitung here at Blooper's for a chat with the latest Pink Party candidate," said the mousy reporter, pushing a microphone at Mrs. Blooper who looked like a flustered walrus wearing a shocking-pink wig and a campaign button that said "Blooper for Mayoress of Elsinore."

The purchase-the-perfect-pooper-scooper jingle came on, and Lindsey switched off the TV. She heard her stomach growl just as Jeeves rapped at the door, carrying in a tureen of consommé.

"Isn't there any solid food in the house?" she asked. After a week of soft foods, she was ready to go into the garden and yowl along with the stray animals.

Jeeves glanced over his shoulder to make sure nobody could hear. "There's some peanut brittle Miss Prymm hides in the kitchen. She *chews*, you know."

"Could you please bring me some?"

A voice calling Lindsey's name shot through the window, and she saw Zach up in the air riding on a snazzy, chrome-plated blimp, sleek as a rubber shark, and roofless because the top had been scooped out and fitted with four bucket seats.

Lindsey waved excitedly. She grabbed a cotton jacket and hurried down to the front porch.

"Wanna come for a ride?" said he.

"Sure!" she exclaimed, shedding every trace of feminine mystique. "Where did you get the blimp?"

"My great-great grandfather. I got it for the rest of the day."

"How does it work?" she asked. There didn't seem to be any steering wheel.

"It's a kind of airship – a dumbot pilot's down in front and the motor's in the back," said Zach. "All I gotta do is type commands into the dashboard or yell into the speaker, and we go where we want."

"Wow!"

"Get in," he said.

A sliding panel vanished into the side of the blimp, opening an entrance with a narrow, herring-bone staircase that led up to the passenger seats.

"Lindsey," demanded Marie Celeste, striding out the door, "what's going on here?"

"Nothing."

"Let me introduce myself to you, Madame," said Zach silkily. "I am the great-great grandson of Chief Constable Dogberry. I'm honored to meet you."

"A gentleman," noted Marie Celeste. "It's always a pleasure to receive a gentleman caller. Lesson eight."

"May I humbly request the privilege of escorting you ladies up for a breath of air?" inquired Zach, laying it on thick.

"Thank you, you lovely boy," oozed Marie Celeste, "but air travel can be hazardous to the digestive tract. With my delicate constitution, I prefer to keep my feet on the ground. It helps one to age gracefully."

"Ahhh." Zach exuded charm. "So that's your secret."

"Where are your manners, Lindsey? You mustn't leave your guest dangling in the air like a rhetorical question. Ask him in."

71

"But dear Aunt Marie Celeste," said Lindsey, latching onto the mood, "I'm reluctant to turn down his kind invitation lest I hurt his feelings."

"An admirable sentiment," concurred the aunt. "The Dogberrys aren't going to vote for Poochinda Blooper, are they?"

"I really can't say." Zach's smile was reaching the cracking point.

"All right, Lindsey, my dear. As long as tiglons can't fly, you should be safe enough. Be sure to get home in time for dinner. We're having sauté of sushi soup and –"

"See you later," said Lindsey. She hopped aboard and climbed into the seat beside Zach.

"And do invite your young gentleman to join us."

"Sure thing," said Lindsey. "Bye."

"*Au revoir*, Lindsey," said Marie Celeste, bidding them goodbye in her best French. "*Au revoir*, Mr. Dogberry."

"The name is Bond," said the boy. "Zachary Bond."

*

Lindsey gazed down at Elsinore. "Can we go to McSolid's Food Factory?" she asked.

"You mean Maxi's. That's what us kids call it."

"If I don't get some solid food fast –"

"First I wanna take you to Arden Forest."

Lindsey wondered what kid in his right mind would ask Marie Celeste along. She scrutinized Zach's face. "How come you invited her?"

"I knew she wouldn't come. The old girl's scared of flying. She never even sets foot on her King Lear jet except when it's parked on the runway. She likes to inspect the refrigerator."

"Why would she buy a plane if she doesn't fly?"

"To bring in voters," said he.

"It must cost a fortune."

"Yeah, really big bucks. The oldies call it 'the price of freedom.' Jack's looking for a way to cash in."

It was a heady sensation to be soaring over the treetops with a hunky-looking boy like Zach. The wind brushed back her hair and made her tingle. She zipped up her jacket and wrapped it around her tightly, wondering if this glorious feeling was anything like falling in love.

The blimp turned southeast and floated along the coast. Below them, dolphins played dodge ball with a ripe coconut, and sea lions dived off a rocky stretch into pools of swirling foam.

"It's so fabulous here," said Lindsey, spellbound.

Zach's fingers crept around her waist, breaking the spell. She slipped his grip. The expression on his face was so total dork that she suddenly felt like walloping him. Instead, she turned away.

"What's that?" she asked, indicating a distant fortress.

"Dogberry's Retreat. I live there."

As they approached it, a huge sign came into view: ARDEN REIN FOREST – 1/4 MILE A HEDD.

"It rains a lot?"

"Nah. One of Quayle's dumbots painted the sign."

"That one too?" She pointed at a clumsily lettered billboard that read:

MUGWUMP'S ARTIFICIAL BARRIERS
walls, fences, gates, barricades, blockades
& made-to-order borders –
conveniently located at our Wall Street showroom
"WHEN THE GOING GETS TOUGH
THE TOUGH GET FENCES!"

Zach pulled a blank. He read it aloud twice and said, "Mugwump's?"

"Maxiiiiiii's," she wailed.

"Sure thing." His eyes, murky as sinkholes, almost hypnotized her. He was oh-so-handsome it made her dimples quiver.

Zach logged in the command, and the blimp turned northward. Near the edge of Arden Forest, they flew over a two-story bungalow painted a bilious shade of pink.

"What's that?"

"Elsinore Prison. My great-great grandpa's on duty there. He doesn't trust the robots. He's got some big-shot prisoner in the clink."

"In the clink?" All at once she remembered the myna bird. "Any idea what 'Rose pink in the clink' means?"

Zach scratched the top of his head until he was sure she'd noticed his biceps bulging under his polo shirt.

"Could be the name of a prisoner?" she asked.

"Dunno. The oldies never tell us anything."

"Maybe we can find out by ourselves," she said. "Let's take a look."

They flew in closer. The prison windows were shuttered and barred. Inside the prison yard, the renegade tiglon reared and roared in agony. It was a magnificent beast and a very angry one indeed.

"We'd better report we've sighted the missing tiglon," said Lindsey, reaching for her walkie-talkie.

"What about the ban? Nobody's allowed to –"

"Let's try. Mayday! Mayday!" she called.

The mini-screen lit up displaying a picture of a blue glove wagging its index finger. "Your call is definitely important to us," announced Mayor Mandher's voice, "but we're not going to answer it. Watch out or we'll conflagrate your walkie-talkie. Have a good day."

"Told you so," said Zach.

A ferocious roar shattered the air. They leaned out and studied the tiglon as it pawed at the prison bars.

"If your great-great grandfather's inside, he must have heard it," observed Lindsey, "but nobody's making a move."

"I bet the wall's too thick."

Maybe Dogberry's too thick, she thought. Or maybe he's just as scared as the other oldies.

Zach broke into a rash of goose bumps. "What an animal!"

"It's cross-bred between a tiger and a lion," said she, glad that her father had taught her so much about wildlife. "They're very rare."

"And hard to catch," he added.

"Doesn't look like they're trying too hard."

"If they don't catch it soon, they'll have to postpone the elections again. Lots of oldies are scared of flying."

"Come off it, Zach, you give a hoot about the elections?"

"Nah, but I kinda hope the Pinks win. Ever been to the Pink Zone? That's where all the excitement is. Wanna go now?"

"Maxiiiiiii's!"

"Right." He snapped his fingers, and off they flew to Maxi's dome. They landed gently but stirred up enough air to disturb the flamingo from her perch in the satellite dish.

"SKEEWAAHKKK!" protested the bird.

"Easy does it, old girl," said Zach.

The flamingo settled herself back into her nest and gazed lovingly into his eyes. Another quick conquest for young Mr. Bond.

"Lindsey, I've got to pick up my brother and another kid. Get yourself some chow. I'll be back in a snap."

Lindsey went downstairs. The only client in the place was Ryan who was at a computer pounding away at the keyboard, a platter of raw celery and carrots beside him. He greeted her with a limp wave of the hand.

"Ryan, you're on a diet or something?"

"You think I'm too fat?"

Was he serious? Judging from the pained expression in his eyes, he needed some reassurance, so she made a show of looking him over. His face was round enough to make him appear pudgy, and the contours of his body were softly molded as if he'd been growing too fast to replace all his baby fat with muscle, but she'd hardly call him fat.

"No," she said. "Just wondering why you're eating celery and carrots."

"Hardest food they've got," said he, passing her a whale-shaped menu. "I'm worried my teeth might atrophy from disuse."

"Your Aunt Sally doesn't give you solids anymore?"

"She can't. The old face-bracer is home all the time – too chicken to go out. So, it's porridge and pudding every day." He glumly selected a stalk of celery and bit in.

"How did you get here?"

"My aunt dropped me off. Unkie's in the cellar drilling his bodyguards on political protectionism or something like that. He thinks I'm up in my room watching TV." Ryan pushed the platter toward her, and she went for it. Nothing had ever tasted as good as a raw carrot.

"Let's get some real food," he said.

They caught the dumbot's attention and ordered burgers and Maxi's fresh-squeezed fruit fraps.

"Find out anything?" she asked. The computer screen was aglow with fiery volcanoes spouting molten lava.

"I searched Jedgar. There's got to be a million entries – some kind of super-secret, counter-espionage organization with a license to kill."

Lindsey helped herself to another carrot. The crunchiness was invigorating. "Can't be much of a secret if there's a million entries. And what's it got to do with the Inferno anyway?"

"Probably a coincidence. So I searched volcanoes. Been online all morning. I just might be the world's greatest expert on live volcanoes. Ask me anything, the speed lava moves –"

"Lotta good that does. Let me check my e-mail." She took over the computer and found several messages from her father. And pictures. She printed them out and dashed off a quick response.

By the time the dumbot brought the food, her stomach was ready to start yodeling. She slipped into place across from Ryan and ate hungrily while he plied her with questions. She didn't have much to report, but between mouthfuls she gave him what little information she'd picked up. He was particularly keen to hear about the tiglon in the Elsinore Prison yard.

"Any ideas?" she asked.

"Yeah, Billy the Bard is the key." He smiled knowingly.

"What's that supposed to mean?"

"If my theory is correct," said Ryan, "we'll be able to figure things out when we find out why all the oldies are so mental about William Shakespeare."

"All the oldies? Even your uncle?"

"Uh-huh. What about your aunt?"

"It's the only book in the whole house."

"See!"

"Your uncle's a poetry freak?" she said, unable to think of anybody who looked less poetic.

"Absolutely. Every time he passes my room he yells, 'How sharper than a serpent's tooth it is to have a thankless child!' That's from Shakespeare."

"It is?"

He nodded. "From a play called *King Lear*. Unkie knows all the lines about teeth."

"How come you know it's Shakespeare? You memorized the whole book?"

"Sure did. What did you do all week? Watch TV?"

Lindsey was stung. She wasn't about to admit how much time she'd wasted watching TV and playing checkers with Jeeves.

Eager to change the subject, she said, "Let's look him up."

"Already did."

Ryan took a deep breath and began reciting: "William Shakespeare lived from 1564 to 1616. Born in the small town of Stratford-upon-Avon, in Warwickshire, England, Shakespeare grew up to be a renowned actor, director, poet, and playwright. Universally hailed as the foremost writer in the English language and the world's top dramatist, he is often called 'The Bard of Avon,' or simply 'The Bard,' which means the poet. His surviving works, translated into every major language, consist of 38 plays, 154 sonnets, two lengthy narrative poems –"

"Get a load who's here!" A strident voice and a clomping of footsteps reverberated down the staircase and Jack, alias the Jackerman, joined them.

"Hiya," said Lindsey.

"Hey!" Jack flashed a metallic grin at Ryan as if noticing him for the first time. "I know you. Yes, sirree, I know you. You were in school with me a couple of years ago. In Washington."

"Maybe you're thinking of somebody else," said Ryan, grasping a thread of hope. "I live in Chicago."

"Yeah, but you used to live in D.C. The kids at school used to call you –"

"Shut up!" yelled Ryan.

"Your nickname was –"

"Shut up!" Ryan's complexion grew thunderous. Neck veins throbbing, he rose to confront Jack.

"What'll you give me if I shut up?" said Jack.

"I'll clobber you if you don't!"

This is unreal, thought Lindsey, a cream-puff kid like Ryan suddenly going ballistic. She somehow couldn't picture him throwing a punch – he was too brainy for that. And Jack, who was half his size, didn't look particularly worried.

"Strictly a business proposition," said Jack, crossing his heart. "If the price is right, your secret's safe."

"What's his nickname?" asked Lindsey.

"Awww, give me a break," groaned Ryan. He crumpled back into his seat.

"I'm a pro and a deal's a deal," said Jack. "Ready to pay, Egghead?"

"Will you shut up for a hamburger?"

"Got any dirty pictures?" asked Jack.

"No," said Ryan, registering his disgust.

The Jackerman eyed Ryan's pocket. "Whatcha got in there?"

"Baseball cards." Ryan pulled out a small stack.

"Let me see." Jack thumbed through the cards. "Okay, I guess it's a deal. You treat, and I eat."

He pushed his way into the booth and snapped his fingers. A dumbot padded over.

"Get me two double-cheese maxi-burgers, a jumbo basket of fries, two giant root beers, and some chocolate chip cookies. No more baby food for me," said Jack.

Tooting under its breath, the dumbot vanished into the kitchen.

"And bring us three chocolate ice-cream sodas for starters. I hate to drink alone."

"Know something, Jack, you're a little creep, and sooner or later you're going to pay for this," said Ryan.

Jack laughed. "Nothing personal."

"Why don't you just tell people your nickname? Otherwise he'll keep on blackmailing you forever," said Lindsey.

"If he opens his mouth, he's a goner," said Ryan sullenly.

"Not to worry, you're in the presence of a first-class spy." Jack slung his elbows over the back of the booth and looked around impatiently.

After a long wait, the dumbot shuffled out of the kitchen, took the tray over to the cash register, and began itemizing the bill. Jack jumped up, snatched the tray, piled the food in front of himself, and dug in.

"Hey, Carrot Head, pass the veggies," he said to Lindsey.

Rather than wait two seconds, he leaned across her, grabbed the ketchup, and doused the buns. A red glob dribbled over the edge and splattered his shirt. Unfazed, he wiped the stains with a plump fry and popped it into his mouth.

"I've seen goats with better table manners," said Ryan.

Lindsey giggled, "I know the perfect place to get him etiquette lessons."

Jack was immune to criticism. He licked his fingers and attacked the burger, and Lindsey couldn't believe that such a skinny kid could pack away so much food. Maybe he'd ordered some of it for his brother.

"That reminds me," she said, "where's Zach? I thought he was picking you up."

"HAR, HAR! Eat your heart out – Romeo's got a date with Cerise. I've got Miss Prymm's private blimp. I know a couple of things about her she'd rather keep hushed up."

If Jack hoped to stir any envy, he'd bungled it. He looked at the others and saw that he wasn't impressing anyone. Ryan eyeballed him balefully, and Lindsey simmered to a boil.

Three long faces bent out of shape, and not a word was spoken for a full ten minutes. The dumbot switched on an old-fashioned jukebox, and they listened to the songs, swallowed their solids, sipped their sodas, and glowered.

Chapter Ten

LEADERSHIP QUALITIES

"We're here!" The Barbie doll breezed down the stairs, her hair billowing. "Hi, y'all. I'm Cerise, and I'm a Virgo. My boyfriend Zachary is a Capricorn."

"Hi, y'all," mimicked Lindsey. "I'm Lindsey, and I'm a Leo."

"Ryan. Total Libra."

"Remember me? Jack the Scorpio."

"Zachary Bond," called Cerise, "what's taking so long up there?"

Zach's voice echoed from the rooftop. "Gotta hitch up the blimp so it won't blow away."

"Isn't it grand all of us here together in Paradise?" bubbled Cerise. "I just love it. So thrilling. All I need is a nice little steak sandwich to be perfectly happy."

Lindsey couldn't take her eyes off her. Unlike California girls, Cerise looked fluffy. Her fly-away hair, her fluttery eyelashes, her ruffled peasant blouse – everything about her was in motion right down to the pompoms on her shoe laces. And her coloring was so peachy-creamy that Lindsey suspected she was wearing blusher. Unable to make up her mind if the girl was for real or what, Lindsey settled in to catch the performance.

A dumbot in a cowboy suit sidled up to Cerise, and she placed an order of steak sandwiches for herself and Zach. "Medium rare, if you please, Sir," she told the dumbot.

It stared blankly. Ryan snapped his fingers, and the dumbot obeyed.

Zach came down the stairs and squeezed into the booth with Cerise. She was all smiles, but the general mood was far from friendly. The five mutely sized each other up.

"How old are you?" Cerise asked Ryan.

"Almost twelve."

"So you're still eleven. Only a year older than my little squirt brother," said Zach, working out the arithmetic.

"Sure, but I'm going into ninth grade. How about you?"

"Seventh grade," said Zach.

Cerise batted her eyes at Ryan. "You skipped a grade?"

"Twice," said Ryan. He folded his arms over his chest.

The dumbot rounded the table to serve the newcomers, and Jack caught its sleeve.

"Another soda for me," he said, pressing his luck, "and put it on Ryan's bill."

Making a mental note to even the score at the first opportunity, Ryan ignored Jack and swept his eyes around the group.

"I've got something to say to you, guys," he began, "and it's important. We're living in the shadow of a monstrous volcano that could wipe us out any minute, and the oldies are all too loony to do anything about it."

"My Great Granny Ellis says there is no volcano," said Cerise.

"She's crazy as a coot," said Jack.

"She's the sweetest little old thing, and she's real nice to me — and my canary," pouted Cerise. "And I don't think y'all should say anything bad about her."

"Notice anything strange about her, Cerise?" asked Ryan.

"Well, she just loves to dance. She's got herself seven real cute little dumbots, and she square-dances with them at night and keeps me awake."

"The old girl's off her rocker," said Zach. "Thinks she's Snow White with the seven dwarfs."

"Does everybody agree that all the oldies are crazy?" asked Ryan.

He heard minor grumbling, but no argument.

"So," he continued, "we're within a few miles of a humungous active volcano, and none of the oldies admit it exists. No evacuation plans, no gas masks, no nothing. Last week's eruption wasn't even mentioned in the news. Poochie Blooper was the lead story."

The kids squirmed in their seats waiting for Ryan to go on.

"There's something called a Jedgar," he said. "Who's heard of it?"

They all had.

"Anybody know what it is?" he asked.

Nobody did.

"I think we'd better crack the mystery and figure out what to do before we all get killed," said Ryan.

Jack moved into his face. "Knock it off. Mount Cinderella's pretty far away –"

"Think so? Ever see pictures of what happened to Pompeii when Mount Vesuvius erupted? In an area covering hundreds of square miles, the whole population got buried alive. That was over 2000 years ago, and they're still digging up bodies."

Ryan paused while the others exchanged worried glances.

Cerise slid closer to Zach and whispered, "He's scarin' me."

"Are we the only kids on Elsinore?" asked Lindsey.

"No," said Jack. "There's some on the far side of the Pink Zone. Whale's Jaw peninsula."

Cerise looked baffled. "How do you know?"

"It's my business to know," said Jack. He leaned over and swiped the pickle from her plate.

"We'd better team up and recruit them. There might be real trouble ahead," said Ryan.

Zach tore his paper napkin into five pieces and handed out the scraps. "Let's choose a leader. Everybody write down a name. Secret ballot."

Cerise passed a pencil around, and they took turns writing. She and Lindsey voted for Zach. Zach voted for himself. Ryan voted for Lindsey. And Jack left his ballot blank, hoping to become the tie breaker. They rolled the ballots into balls and tossed them onto the Formica table. Three out of five gave Zach the majority.

Lindsey mentioned that it would show solidarity if they made the vote unanimous, and Ryan agreed. He retrieved his ballot, crossed out Lindsey's name, and wrote in Zach's. But Jack wasn't buying it. No way he'd put up with Romeo as a leader.

"I quit!" he announced, rising to his feet like an exclamation point.

"Spoil sport, dirty wart. We don't need you anyway," chanted Cerise.

"Yes, we do," said Ryan. "Like it or lump it, we've gotta have a good spy."

They'd reached a stalemate, and Jack was gloating. It burned Lindsey that one little brat could impose his will on the whole group. She half wished they'd just get rid of him, but with so few kids on Elsinore they could hardly afford to lose a member of the think tank.

Ryan suggested that they hold a yes/no vote, and he proposed Lindsey, who felt so flattered that she decided to vote for herself. They tore up another napkin and cast their ballots. The count was four yeses and one no.

"She wins," said Ryan.

"I think the chairman should be a boy," objected Cerise. "I mean, we can't call her the chair*man* if she's a girl, can we?"

"That's the dumbest thing I've ever heard," said Jack.

Total airhead, thought Lindsey, and she found herself wondering if Cerise had a problem with that feminine mystique business.

"Would it make any difference to you if we call her the chair-*woman*?" asked Ryan, making an effort to be patient.

"But she *isn't* a woman," said Cerise. "And I'm older than she is, aren't I? And I think the leader should be a boy."

"Tough break, Carrot Head," said Jack.

"Which means you've just disqualified yourself, Cerisy," said Lindsey, her eyes blazing.

The only candidates left were Jack and Ryan, but Zach promptly vetoed his brother, so it was Ryan or nobody.

"Who'll vote for Ryan?" asked Lindsey. All hands went up.

"Congratulations, Fatso," said Jack. "Keep on winning elections and you might grow up to be a bigwig like your uncle."

Lindsey was so fed up with Jack that she pounced on him. "Don't you dare call him fat," she seethed, "just because you look like a scarecrow!"

"Let's get organized," said Ryan, and he proposed that they set up a task force and divvy up the assignments. The idea made sense to Lindsey, but Jack hadn't finished running interference. He started bellyaching that they had to have a secret code name first. According to him, no self-respecting spy organization could operate without a code name.

In the argument that followed, Zach unexpectedly sided with his brother claiming that everybody in Washington, D.C., even cats and dogs, had a secret code name. It was two against two until Cerise tipped the scales in favor of the Bonds.

"My canary has a code name," she said. "I call him Birdie."

They brainstormed. Cerise suggested that they call themselves "The Blue Brigade," but they scrapped the idea when Zach remembered it was the name of the local police force, and they might get into trouble for impersonating officers. Jack thought they should call themselves "The Super Spy Stinger Squad," which he claimed was both original and brilliant. He pushed hard but couldn't sway anyone. After a great deal of debate, Lindsey came up with "Ryan's Rangers." They all liked the sound of it, and a murmur of approval greeted the suggestion.

Ryan retook the floor to announce that he'd be holding a meeting same time, same place, every day until further notice. He told the Rangers to compose question lists and bring them to the next meeting.

"What kind of questions?" asked Cerise.

"For example," said Ryan, "why there are so many blackouts."

"Oh, I don't know." Cerise looked around helplessly.

"Boy, is she dumb!" exclaimed Jack.

"She was smart enough to figure out that we don't need *you*," said Ryan. "Any more insults and you're out."

"Right," said Zach, wishing he'd said that.

"I've got a question for Ryan: how come your Uncle Jerry always wears gloves?" asked Lindsey.

Ryan cracked up. "Because his hands look like mince-meat. They're covered with scars. He hasn't got a square inch of skin that doesn't look mangled."

"Your uncle's a war hero?" asked Cerise.

"An orthodontist," he laughed. "Got himself bitten all the time. There was one itsy-bitsy little third-grade girl with an overbite like a camel who really got him. He was trying to pound a Jerk the Jaw Jammer into her mouth. She took one look at it and went bananas. Before he knew it, she clamped her teeth onto his fingers and bit right down to the bone. Nearly took his knuckles off. He shook her until her adenoids rattled, but she wouldn't let go. The hygienist had to give her four doses of ether before they could peel her off."

Lindsey grinned, "I guess that'd discourage anybody from letting kids chew."

"What a sorrowful story," said Cerise.

The meeting was breaking up, but Lindsey wasn't ready to go home. She suggested that if it wasn't too late they could visit the Pink Zone and try to locate the missing kids.

To her annoyance, Jack pushed his Electronic Epsilon Delux iiiWatch at her and said, "It's exactly four twenty-two."

"How about it, guys?" said Ryan.

"No hassle," said Zach. "I've got the blimp all day. Hey, Squirt, where did you see those kids?"

Jack marked an X on the jaw of the whale-shaped menu and passed it to Zach, who stuffed it into his pocket.

Cerise glared at him. "Zachary Bond, you said you'd take me to choir practice."

"Where's that?" asked Ryan.

"Isosceles Square," said Zach, "opposite the Globe Theatre."

Ryan was growing curious. "What kind of church is it, Cerise?" he asked.

"I don't know, Ryan. All I do is sing."

"Would you find out from your great grandmother? It might be important. Some kind of oddball cult …. Okay, guys, let's get going."

Cerise's voice climbed to a treble. "What about my ride!"

Zach elbowed his brother and gave him a knowing look.

"I'll drop her off. I've got some investigating to do in the White Zone," said Jack, abruptly getting up to leave.

Cerise flounced out after him without so much as a lukewarm "good-bye."

Chapter Eleven

RANGERS AND STRANGERS

Ryan, Lindsey, and Zach programmed the blimp for a flight into the Pink Zone. Gentle gusts carried them over the rooftops. Jasmine perfumed the air and soft breezes rose from the sea to cool their cheeks.

Lindsey looked back to enjoy a bird's eye view of Elsinore Harbor. Hundreds of pleasure boats perched on the waves. Arks, speedboats, catamarans, galleons, kayaks, canoes, houseboats, and rafts crowded the port in a zigzag formation. She picked out a sleek little boat and imagined herself sailing into the wind.

Ryan let off a sigh, his eyes lingering on a distant water-skier, and Lindsey realized that he too was yearning to have some fun.

An electric-blue jet seared the sky, and Lindsey wondered if it was Captain Friedman. She hadn't thought about him for a while, nor had she bothered to phone him. By now she'd become completely absorbed with life on Pensioners' Paradise. Even if he suddenly showed up and offered her a flight out, she wasn't about to go. She cared about Elsinore and her new friends. How would she feel, she asked herself, if she copped out on the Rangers?

Zach broke into her reverie. "Hey, Lindsey, I just thought of a question. Is there something wrong with your name?"

"What's in a name?" said Ryan, still annoyed that they'd wasted so much of the meeting fighting over a code name.

"I mean, when I told my great-great grandparents I really liked a girl named Rosalind, they went mental."

"No kidding?" said Lindsey. "When my great aunt heard it, her eyes nearly popped out of her head."

They both looked to Ryan, and he answered as if thinking

out loud. "Well, Rosalind is the name of a character in a Shakespeare play."

"So that's why." Zach seemed satisfied.

"But if my theory is correct," continued Ryan, "Shakespeare is what unites the oldies, not what divides them. They're all bonkers over Shakespeare, so it stands to reason that they should all go for the name Rosalind."

Lindsey said, "Maybe it's the 'Rosa' part. In San Diego some people say "rosa" to mean pink. The Dogberrys are Blues?"

"Right." Zach draped his arm over Lindsey's shoulder. "You know, Ryan, I'm kinda glad you won. It leaves me more time for other things."

Lindsey brushed the arm away. "Cut it out!"

"I like redheads. They've got spunk," he grinned.

"Leave her alone, Zach. We've got to work as a team."

So, the big bad wolf left the little redhead riding undisturbed – for the time being.

*

Before long, they left behind the center of town and headed inland until they found themselves floating over Rosé Raceway, the only paved road in the Pink Zone. To Lindsey's surprise, the scenery underwent a dramatic change. As if at a brush stroke, flowering treetops burst into brightness. No more to be seen were the trim lawns, the sedate mansions, or the imposing office buildings with their cookie-cutter regularity. Instead, the architecture was a hodge-podge of shapes and colors.

Here people lived in windmills, boxcars, teepees, circus tents, ivory towers, adobe huts, log cabins, glass-domed gazebos, and igloos made of dry ice. The homes were painted in shimmering sherbet shades—raspberry, peach, and watermelon — or else with stripes, checks, polka-dots, and plaids. One flat-topped roof was decorated with a tic-tac-toe design, and a party of oldies was taking turns hopping on the squares.

It was hard to tell where anybody's property started or ended. Playing fields, game parks, and swimming pools dotted the hills and valleys. Unweeded gardens dipped into unfenced pastures where animals grazed unmolested. Oldies hiked along unmarked trails past bubbling brooks and orchards where squealing monkeys raided the fruit, and life rolled on as freely as if nobody had ever heard of Mayor-Shall-Rule.

Lindsey took in the limitless playground. "It looks like Animal Kingdom down there," she said wistfully.

"Let's head for the amusement park," said Zach, thinking of the tunnel of love. "The kids who live here really got it made. There's a water world at Walden Pond —"

"I hate to be a kill-joy," interrupted Ryan, "but we're supposed to be checking out the place where Jack saw those kids."

Using the menu as a road map, they traveled southward to the underbelly of the whale-shaped island and turned eastward over a deserted peninsula, a stretch of land with nothing on it but gaggles of gooney birds clacking along the sand bars.

They came to a billboard that read: THE FOUR KIDS' COMMUNICATIONS CONGLOMERATE

Underneath it in boldfaced characters were the logo K⁴CC and a warning: DO NOT ENTER!

"Those kids you met at the airport might live out here," suggested Lindsey even though there were no houses in sight. "What about the sign? You think we should ignore it?"

"It doesn't say *danger*," said Ryan. "It could be private property. Trespassing on air space —"

"Forget the stupid sign. There are times we gotta go above the law," said Zach, flexing his muscles.

Lindsey eyed him skeptically. It sounded to her as if he were repeating something he'd overheard an adult say, probably his great-great grandfather. Dogberry was the law in Elsinore.

Ryan gave the command, and they continued floating along the barren peninsula. After about a mile, they spotted a lone building in the middle of a wasteland plateau, a concrete structure shaped like a crucifix with four wings that spread out at right angles from a central courtyard. The longest extension was labeled "Richie Gatz." The three shorter ones were labeled in turn "Chip Appleby," "Oscar Spielman," and "Rhett Turnerov." A pink, white, and blue banner with the K⁴CC logo was flying from a flagpole.

"See that?" Zach indicated a partially canopied courtyard in the center of the cross. Sprawling on the lawn under an apple tree, a long-legged boy was busily dismantling a laptop computer. His face was hidden behind a sweep of straight brown hair.

"Prepare for landing," said Ryan, and the blimp slowly descended.

"You recognize him?" asked Lindsey.

"Yeah." Ryan hung out and waved. "Hey, Richie, remember me?"

The boy looked up and shouted, "Don't come any closer! Stay where you are!"

"We want to talk to you!"

An alarm went off and Zach freaked. He signaled wildly with both arms, letting the menu slip through his fingers. It floated away like a fish tossed by the currents. As it brushed the treetops, it tripped a beam and set off a network of electrical charges. The cardboard crumpled at the edges, burst into flames, and blackened. Within seconds all that remained was the faint smell of smoke.

Zach looked sick. "That could have been me!"

"Hold on!" cried Richie. "Chip, hey, Chipper! Deactivate the system!"

A garage window overlooking the courtyard suddenly swung open, and another lanky, brown-haired kid appeared. He yanked a lever and shut down the network.

"It's safe to land," called Richie. He lay back on his elbows and watched unperturbed as the Rangers alighted.

"What was that?" asked Ryan as he hopped out of the blimp.

"Our security system. Sorry to inconvenience you," said Richie, his formality in sharp contrast with his sloppy appearance.

The boy named Chip stepped out of the garage and joined them. "You almost got yourselves fried," he said pleasantly. "We weren't expecting guests."

Zach was still in shock. "You need all that security? You nearly electrocuted me!"

"Not enough power for that. Might have singed your hair," smiled Chip. He opened a package of sunflower seeds and began popping them into his mouth.

Ryan introduced Lindsey and Zach, and they all took places on a carpet of grass.

"Whaddya think of K⁴CC? Want me to show you around?" asked Chip.

"Maybe later," said Ryan, but Chip wasn't listening.

He clicked off a screen saver, and the stained-glass windows along Richie's wing went transparent, revealing a supersonic laboratory humming with activity. Lindsey swept her eyes around the complex. Through the windows, she could pick out teams of workers moving purposefully through a maze of computing machines.

"This place is yours?" she asked.

"Most of it's mine," said Richie with a proprietary air. "Basically, it's a learning center. You could say it's our brainchild. Think of it as a home school where the students are the teachers. It's all about the future, and we're it — not that all the oldies appreciate us."

"Every time they see us, they pass a new law," grumbled Chip. "I'm not going into town anymore." He tossed another sunflower seed into his mouth. His eyes glazed over with contentment as he gulped it down.

"Chip and I live here," said Richie. "The others just show up for the summer."

"The others?" said Lindsey.

"Oscar and Rhett, the other two members of K⁴CC," he said.

"Ryan thought you disappeared from the airport," she told Richie.

He shook his head. "We took a mini-vacation, but we're usually here."

So nobody's missing, and no kids are being held hostage on Elsinore, thought Lindsey. She shot Ryan a look that said, "Were you wrong or what!"

Ryan winced. "I saw your names crossed out."

"Where?" asked Richie.

"The visitors' register."

Richie burst out laughing. "No wonder. The immigration lady is so flaky — always forgets we're not visitors, we're permanents. Every time we land, she goes into her 'recite-your-poem' routine."

"Ryan thought something had happened to you," said Lindsey.
"You were worried about us?" Richie assumed a mocking tone. "Awww, that's so sweet."

Ryan nearly choked. He quickly changed the subject by asking them about Jedgar's Inferno. Richie had never heard of it, but Chip suddenly looked alert.

"What kind of computer is that?" he asked.

Unbelievable, thought Lindsey, what a pair of geeks!

It turned out that they were geeks all right, the child prodigies who had dreamed up most of the technology that the oldies used. K⁴CC was their private play station, where they dwelled like young gods.

Lindsey realized she was witnessing a miracle of advanced technology, and she suddenly felt bowled over. It was awesome to see what kids her age had managed to create through sheer brainpower. But geeks or no geeks, she reasoned, nobody could be *that* out of it. They had to know something about the Inferno. It dawned on her that if the Rangers could tap their know-how, maybe Pensioners' Paradise could be made safe.

Ryan started grilling the geeks about Mount Cinderella, and Richie looked mildly interested. He said he'd flown past it plenty of times and never noticed anything wrong. After some prodding, he admitted that he usually couldn't be bothered to look out the window, but he claimed that Oscar and Rhett were out filming the whole area. In his opinion, they were the ones to talk to.

Chip thrust his hand into the bag of sunflowers seeds, discovered it was empty, and realized that his stomach was empty too.

"Must be lunchtime," he said, absent-mindedly consulting his iiiWatch. It was an Electronic Epsilon Delux.

"Where'd you get that watch?" asked Lindsey.

Chip permitted himself a spacey smile. "I invented it. It runs on a microchip the size of a grain of rice, and it's got over four thousand cyber-space-linked functions. There's only two of its kind in the whole world." He knitted his eyebrows. "I got weaseled out of the other one by a kid who was trying to rip off my patent."

"Oh," said she.

Ryan was eager to get back to basics. He zeroed in on Richie, who answered a few questions before getting defensive. Floods and blackouts weren't his fault, he claimed, and they hadn't affected K⁴CC. He liked to mind his own business, and he was sick of hearing about the Pinks and the Blues and all the stupid problems they caused. Why couldn't everybody just leave him in peace to work on his projects? His voice was cool, but his body language was screaming, "Get off my case!"

"You don't care what happens to us?" cried Lindsey. "You're heartless!"

Neither Richie nor Chip reacted, and she wondered if they had any feelings at all. Brainy as they were, it looked as if they had no clue about the golden mean. If there was one thing she'd learned from her mother, it was that hearts and minds had to work together, and it occurred to her that the kids at K⁴CC might not be human.

She fixed them with an angry look. "You're robots?"

"What's this all about anyway?" asked Richie. "I'm not looking for any more grief. I've got bundles of trouble around here."

"There's something called a Jedgar. We don't know what it is, but we know it's dangerous," said Ryan. "It could kill us all."

That caught Richie's attention. "Could it wipe out K⁴CC?" he asked.

"Maybe, maybe not," said Ryan, and Richie looked almost relieved.

"We need help," added Ryan. "Our survival is at stake, and the oldies are useless. You guys want to join forces?"

"You mean this is for real?" asked Richie.

The geeks swapped apprehensive glances, their Olympian indifference beginning to crack. They shrugged their shoulders and said in one breath, "We're with you."

THRONK! – THRONK! – THRONK! – THRONK!

From the wing labeled "Richie," an insistent hacking reverberated through the window panes.

"Aw, naw!" cried Chip. "I forgot to reactivate the security system!"

"What's that?" asked Lindsey.

KA-THONK! – KA-THONK! – KA-THONK!

A nine-foot-tall bird with a beak like a sledge hammer shattered the stained-glass windows and began butting its way through the door.

"It's Sherman again!" wailed Richie. He sank his face into his hands. "Uncle Sammy's ostrich! It's gone berserk attacking us!"

"SKRWAAAAAHK!" shrieked the ostrich.

It smashed and thrashed till the hinges clattered. Then it pitched itself through the casement, reducing the framework to rubble.

"Stop it, Sherman!" howled Richie.

"Run for cover!" cried Ryan, and the kids ran.

The bird galloped into the courtyard and circled it erratically. In a fit of energy, it torpedoed through the canopy, dragging down the canvas. The trees shook. Apples broke loose from their branches and plummeted to the ground.

"CREEEEEE!" went Sherman.

Biting and pecking, the ostrich tore open a hole in the canvas big enough to poke its head through. It looked around stupidly, teeter-tottered to a standing position, and started chasing its own tail. For no apparent reason, it screeched to a halt, dug its head into the ground, and began kicking up dirt with its talons. Buried to the neck and unable to extract itself, it let off a stifled snort and crumpled into a heap.

A blizzard of soiled feathers filled the air and piles of debris littered the lawn. Richie went for a broom and began sweeping.

Zach was beginning to look sick again. "Is it safe to come out?" he asked from behind a tree.

Richie shrugged. "Uh-huh. Sherman's burned himself out and won't attack again for a while. I don't know what we're gonna do. That pest is reducing K⁴CC to smithereens faster than we can rebuild it. We can't get any work done around here."

"Poor old Sherm," said Chip. "I'll call an ambulance."

"Sure, then the vet releases him and back he comes," griped Richie.

Having cleared a spot, Richie motioned the others to sit. "Say, can you help me get rid of Sherman?"

"Maybe Captain Friedman can help. He's gonzo about birds," said Lindsey. "Do you know him?"

"Our great uncle," groaned Richie. "Who do you think Sherman belongs to? The oldies are all crazy."

"What you guys need is a good strong barricade," said Ryan. "Why don't you try Mugwump's? It's on Wall Street right by Elsinore Prison. You can't miss it. It's got a huge sign that says: WHEN THE GOING GETS TOUGH THE TOUGH GET FENCES."

"Thanks for the tip." Richie entered the information on his keypad and pressed "save."

"Guys, listen, we've all got problems, but the Inferno is top priority," said Ryan. "We've got to formulate a viable plan."

Zach nodded. "Gotta protect ourselves."

"We call ourselves Ryan's Rangers," said Lindsey, "and we're rounding up the kids on Elsinore. Any others living in the Pink Zone?"

"No," said Richie, "just the four of us, but we've got scads of robots working for us. I can put the whole lab at your disposal."

"If Sherman doesn't destroy it first," muttered Chip, inspecting a bruised apple. He dropped to his knees and crawled off to salvage the rest.

"Okay, guys," said Ryan. "I'm calling a Rangers' meeting. Who's got a walkie-talkie?"

"Oscar does," said Richie, "but it's not working. He says he swallowed the transistor."

"Hello?" went Lindsey.

"He's kind of excitable," explained Richie. "Anyhow, he had nobody to call until you guys showed up."

"How come you don't invent your own walkie-talkies?" she asked.

"Are you kidding? The Blue Brigade would shut us down if we tried."

Lindsey looked at the rubble and felt sorry for the geeks. "Want us to help clean up the mess?"

Richie shook his head. "We'll get the robots to do it," he said with a thin smile. "Let me know when you need help. We'll be here."

Something about the look on his face convinced Lindsey that the Rangers could count on him.

"Tell Oscar to get another transistor — he'll be hearing from me," said Ryan.

He snapped his fingers, and the dumbot lowered the blimp to let them aboard. Lindsey, Ryan, and Zach departed, leaving the two new Rangers to their apples and their ostrich.

Chapter Twelve

LIGHT THICKENS

Daybreak brought a brownout. Mount Cinderella had been rumbling all night, sending shock waves through the overloaded power lines just as the weather turned hot and muggy. At Number One Azure Avenue, the air conditioning stalled out, its familiar purr silenced. Elsinore seemed to be holding its breath.

Sticky with sweat, her pajamas clinging like damp tissue paper, Lindsey rolled out of bed to soak in a cool tub and go through her unread e-mails, a stack of printouts from her father with color pictures of animals that he hadn't bothered to label. She recognized some of them — dingoes, kangaroos, and Koala bears — but it seemed like bush country had more strange critters than the Pink Zone, things like bandicoots and dugongs, whatever they were, and even a six-foot-long earthworm, which sounded pretty icky. Unfortunately, he'd never heard of a Jedgar.

Her father's stories about Australia were so funny that she found herself laughing out loud as she read, and the tap water was much bubblier than usual, downright fizzy. It tickled her from her armpits to her toes and made her feel silly. She began to sing, glad that no one could hear:

> Montezuma's Mineral is yummy, yummy, yummy,
> Fifty-seven frothy flavors floating in the tummy!
> Buy a barrel every day, nothing could be better!
> Water, water everywhere, but Montezuma's wetter!

She couldn't shake the song from her head, and she had trouble concentrating until she came to a paragraph that was so riveting she had to read it twice to believe it:

Here's something that will interest you. One of my colleagues rescued a lost puppy. As you'll see from the picture, he looks like a terrier – a cute, friendly, little mutt with wiry fur about the color of your own hair. Everybody's crazy about him, so if you want him, you'd better tell me fast before somebody else claims him. Marie Celeste wrote me that your behavior has been "exemplar," so I'll assume you've earned yourself a dog.

Lindsey whooped with joy. Good old Aunt Marie Celeste! She felt like hugging the woman.

Thumbing back through the pictures, Lindsey came to the one of her dad with a reddish-brown fur ball at his chin. The picture was blurry. At first it looked as if his beard had grown so long and fuzzy that he was showing it off, but on closer inspection she realized he was actually holding a puppy.

She'd barely digested the news when an unpleasant thought struck her: Tiffany hated pets.

Too bad for her, thought Lindsey. Any animal hater who wanted to marry an anthrozoologist was begging for trouble. In Lindsey's opinion, the solution was simple – get rid of Tiffany and keep the dog.

BRHUUUGH – CRRRKKKHHH – BAAABHOOOOM.

The sky crackled and boomed, and the house seemed to bounce like a trampoline. The bath water started splashing and slopped over the sides of the tub onto the mat. She grabbed a towel and skidded across the wet floor, which was bucking so hard that she had to hold onto the window sill to keep from getting knocked off her feet.

The tremors rose to a crescendo. Tree trunks bent to and fro like limp licorice sticks scraping their uppermost branches against the lawn. The wrought-iron fence uprooted, flipped over, and flattened the petunia patch, shaking a groundhog from its slumber. The unhappy groundhog poked its nose between blades of grass, turned tail, and darted back into its ditch. Tooting wildly, the lawn elves dropped their tools and dived in after it.

With a final shudder, the quaking subsided, and the noise died out. Lindsey heaved a sigh of relief.

"Sleep no more!" cried Marie Celeste, performing a graceless entry, her hair curled up in Della Robbia blue spoolies, and her bathrobe buttoned into the wrong holes.

"I'm not asleep," said Lindsey, wondering if her aunt would mention the earthquake. It seemed like the list of taboo topics was endless.

"There's a power failure. My television is dead. Heaven knows if we can hold tonight's Blue/Pink debate. I've written the answers, but I haven't had time to decide the questions. I've got a million things to do before the election, and I don't even know if they've caught that wretched tiglon. Oh, how I wish I'd bought a blimp when they were on sale so that I could send you out on errands!"

"Doesn't Miss Prymm have a blimp?" asked Lindsey.

"Soaked through," said the aunt. "Somebody took it to water world and left it under the falls."

Jeeves tapped at the door. "If you please, Madame, I'll serve breakfast right away before the help conks out."

"We'll be down in two minutes, punctually," said the aunt. "I really must call Dr. Mandher. Perhaps he can send his blimp over."

*

Lindsey and her aunt waited on the porch for Ryan to show up.

"I do wish he'd hurry," said Marie Celeste. "Those storm clouds will be reaching us before long."

Lindsey lifted her eyes. In the direction of Jedgar's Inferno, a single black cloud hung like a humungous wig dangling from an invisible hook.

Marie Celeste handed her a satchel. "Take these flyers to Zee Rock's and tell her they have to be redone. I want her to reproduce the serious photos of Dr. Mandher, not the smiling ones," she said. "Some members of our electorate are complaining that his teeth are crooked. And tell Mrs. Rock that if she doesn't print them properly this time, the Blue Party won't pay."

Lindsey took the satchel, grateful for any excuse to go out.

"And don't dawdle. Life is too short to waste time. That's lesson number nine. Ah, here's Ryan."

Ryan was riding high on a plump blimp festooned from nose to tailfins with political slogans. He performed a figure eight in the air, swooped down, and stabilized the blimp alongside the porch (better known as the verandah).

"How much battery time has your dumbot got left?" asked Marie Celeste.

"A couple of hours."

"Be sure to bring Lindsey back before it crashes. And watch out for those clouds. If they start moving in, I don't want you to wind up in any funny neighborhoods."

"No problem," said Ryan. He let Lindsey aboard and lifted off.

"The serious photos with the lips closed," said Marie Celeste. But they were already out of earshot.

*

"I'm calling Oscar," said Ryan, drawing his walkie-talkie from its holster.

"The ban's lifted?" said Lindsey.

"Until nightfall or the next disaster, whichever comes first – Hey, Oscar, it's Ryan."

"Yo!" came a tinselly voice with such a live-wire quality that it sounded as if the transistor might still be stuck in his throat. "I'm joyriding the fallout! Wanna come?"

Lindsey peered at the mini-screen and saw a scruffy looking kid straddling a sky-scooter. Tinted sunglasses and a shock of hair masked the upper part of his face, and the lower part was smudged with pitch, but his mischievous expression was unmistakable. He radiated energy across the screen.

"Any idea how long it'll take before the fallout hits Elsinore?" asked Ryan.

"An hour or two at the rate it's drifting in. Plenty of time to film it."

"Can you double-check with your special effects staff? I want their best estimate. If there's any change, call me."

"Will do."

The image disappeared, and Ryan clipped his walkie-talkie onto his belt.

"Fallout?" asked Lindsey.

"The oldies are calling it a summer squall. Funny coincidence, the black cloud just happens to be coming from the volcano."

"It's erupting again?" She tried to pick out Mount Cinderella, but it was hidden behind fumes. The black wig in the sky was drooping into dreadlocks.

"Not exactly. No flames, fireballs, or lava, but the epicenter of the quake was Jedgar's Inferno."

"Drat that Jedgar," said she. "So the Rangers can't meet today?"

"The air will be too thick with pitch for anybody to travel."

"We'll be grounded again, back to eating mash and mush."

"And slop and glop and gruel."

"You know, Ryan, I'm beginning to really hate pudding. Let's stop by Yung Lu's and stock up on sweet and sour supplies."

"Might be out of business. The Blues are out to zap him."

"How come?"

"Unkie says the place doesn't meet Elsinore's standards for politically correct business practices – or something like that. He's sending Dogberry and the Blue Brigade to shut it down."

"They're making Yung Lu redundant? We've got to warn him."

The more she thought about it, the more her heart bled for the poor old man. He was so proud of his restaurant. She hated to think how devastated he must feel. The least she could do was to *be* there for him. She busied herself trying to find the right words to help him manage his grieving.

"Ryan, if they're shutting the place down," she said emotionally, "it's up to us to help him find closure."

They dropped the flyers off at Zee Rock's Reproductions, placed the new order, and headed for Yung Lu's. As they approached the lighthouse, Lindsey looked down at the harbor and noticed the kitchen help loading crates onto a yacht. Maybe he's already been evicted, she thought sadly.

The Apolitical Asiatic Gourmet Bistro-Teca had seen better days. The earthquake had sunk its seaside front several feet into the sand, and the lighthouse tower was tilting at a ten-degree slant over the beach. As the blimp pulled in for landing, Yung Lu was firing instructions at roving reporter Squeaky Zeitung and a flashy-looking kid with a webcam. Yung Lu was much too preoccupied to notice Lindsey and Ryan until they were almost on top of him.

"You make me feel so Yung," he sang as he welcomed them onto the roof garden.

He was dressed in waterproof fatigues, a crash helmet, and goggles, and he was sporting the largest fanny pack that Lindsey had ever seen. Between the bizarre outfit and the impish grin on his face, he didn't look one bit depressed. Feeling pretty foolish with her sympathetic little speech drying on her tongue, Lindsey introduced Ryan.

"The photography buff?" Yung Lu snapped all ten fingers like castanets. "Fujiyama, bring up the mug shots. And the lunches. The whole shebang."

Lindsey took Yung Lu aside. "Dogberry's coming to shut you down," she said.

"Not until after his noonday nap. By then, I'll be out of here."

"Hey, Boss, that's the mayor's grandson!" crowed Squeaky, his eyes gleaming at Ryan. "Here's a real scoop!"

"Nephew! Not grandson! And leave the kid alone! Come on, let's get rolling."

Yung Lu and Squeaky positioned themselves behind the banquet table. While the unidentified kid adjusted his lens, Lindsey gave him a good looking over.

At first glance, he resembled Richie, Chip, and Oscar except he was so handsome he was almost pretty, a real glamour boy with his hair slicked across his brow. Duded up in a sparkling white baseball uniform rather than jeans, he looked more like a fashion statement than a member of K[4]CC, but Lindsey figured he had to be Rhett.

She asked the kid, "Who are you?"

"Shhh," said Yung Lu. "Roll 'em."

"PPU reporting from Yung Lu's Apolitical Asiatic Gourmet

Bistro-Tech moments before the Blue Brigade sweeps in," announced Squeaky. "Exclusive interview with Elsinore's leading restaurateur."

"Stop the camera, Rhett," said Yung Lu. Then he turned to Squeaky. "Teca! Bistro-Teca makes it sound more exotic! And you forgot to mention it's the finest cuisine on Pensioners' Paradise. *Finest cuisine*! For once in your life, try to get something right."

"Sorry, Boss," said Squeaky.

The camera started rolling again. "Here we are at Yung Lu's, the finest cuisine-cooked food on Pensioners' Paradise. Now here's a statement from Mr. Yung Lu in person," said Squeaky. He passed the mike to Yung Lu, who blossomed before the camera.

"Ladies and gentlemen, I'm proud to announce that by popular demand your favorite downtown restaurant is opening up a new branch on Prospero's Isle. New menu, new venue. You can enjoy our takeout dinners by placing your orders with Maestro Fujiyama –"

"Toot, toot," came a noise from the staircase. The mouth-watering aroma of fancy Asian food filled the air as Fujiyama emerged loaded down with box lunches and a stack of photos.

"Stop the camera," said Yung Lu.

Lindsey was itching with curiosity. She cornered the boy. "You're Rhett? What's going on here?"

"News coverage, Ma'am," he drawled. "Yung Lu's skippin' town before the police nab him."

"Be sure to say 'relocating' not 'skipping town,'" said Squeaky. "Newsmen gotta be accurate."

"May I offer my honored guests a preview of my latest masterpieces?" asked Yung Lu.

Lindsey nodded, and Yung Lu snapped his fingers. "Give me the mug shots and pack up the meal-mobile."

Fujiyama handed him the photos and began piling lunch boxes into Ryan's blimp.

"You'll be the first to sample my hot-to-trot take-out orders," Yung Lu told Lindsey.

She tossed her arms around the old man's neck. "You're wonderful! I'm going to miss you so much! They're really going to arrest you?"

"They've got to catch me first. Nothing like playing hard to get," he chortled.

That's lesson number ten, said Lindsey to herself, suddenly thinking of Zach.

"Take a look at these pictures," beamed Yung Lu. "You like this beauty?" He held out an aerial view of himself bashing Mayor Mandher on the head with a rubber chop stick, and everybody burst out laughing.

"Run it in tomorrow's edition, Squeaky," said Yung Lu, "under the heading 'Political Clout!'"

"Will do, Boss," said Squeaky.

Lindsey asked, "Why does he keep calling him 'Boss'?"

"Don't tell now," whispered Rhett, "Yung Lu owns PPU. And The Elsinore X-Press. What a man!"

Sirens blared. Lindsey, Ryan, Yung Lu, Squeaky, and Rhett hurried to the guardrail and looked out. A fleet of dumbot-drawn wagons screeched into the parking lot and surrounded the lighthouse. Rhett began filming as Dogberry jumped out of his squad car. He was a bulky, barrel-chested oldster with a whiskery spaniel face that sagged into mangy jowls. He looked familiar, and Lindsey wondered where she'd seen him before.

Dogberry took off his ten-gallon hat and waved it at the roof garden. "Open up for the law," he snarled, flashing his canines.

"It's Saturday," Yung Lu called cheerfully. "Business hours don't start until 6:00 p.m."

Dogberry rattled the door handle. "Open up! You're under arrest! I'm Chief Constable Dogberry, and I'm serving you a warrant!"

"Not on my menu," announced Yung Lu. "The specialty of the day is – ha-ha – Noodle Surprise." With that, he grabbed a carton of steaming egg noodles and flung it over the rail. "Surprise!" he shouted.

Dogberry tried to dodge the downpour, but most of the noodles landed on his head and dripped over his shoulders. He furiously wiped his uniform with his knuckles.

"Great shot!" said Rhett, busily filming.

Dogberry was in a perfect snit. He pounded the lighthouse door. "I'll huff and I'll puff and I'll blow the house down!" he blustered. "Bring on the storm troopers!"

Assistant Constable Dull lumbered out of his wagon with the entire Blue Brigade Swat Squad in tow.

"What's going to happen?" asked Lindsey, afraid that Yung Lu might be in for big trouble.

"I'll just have to reinvent myself out west," he smirked. "I'm off to Prospero's Isle!"

The troopers raised a battering ram and charged the entrance. BANG! – BANG! – BANG! The door was beginning to splinter.

"They'll never catch me alive!" yelled Yung Lu. He took a running start, vaulted the guardrail, and coasted to the edge of the roof. With a salute to his friends, he held his nose and leaped.

"No!" cried Lindsey, covering her eyes in horror. She couldn't bear to watch.

"Wowweee!" exclaimed Rhett. "What a man!"

Everybody on the rooftop started clapping. Lindsey opened her eyes and saw Yung Lu's fanny pack bursting into a parachute. He floated toward the yacht, splashed down, and waved good-bye as the crew hauled him on deck. With Yung Lu safely aboard, the yacht sped out of the bay and vanished into the encroaching dreadlocks.

BANG! – BANG! – BANG! The lighthouse door gave way. The troopers broke in and stormed the spiral staircase. Lindsey was too dumbfounded to move.

"We'd better get out of here," said Ryan, pushing her into the blimp. "You guys want a ride?"

"Freedom of the press," squeaked Squeaky. "Count me out – I'm not missing this story."

Rhett nodded. "Me neither. I'm stickin' like grits on a griddle."

Ryan undid the rope and prepared for take-off.

"What about Fujiyama?" asked Lindsey.

The dumbot smiled loftily and went, "Toot."

*

Their blimp loaded with cartons of aromatic egg rolls, fricasseed Formosa rice-patties, stir-fried kiwi, and soy-seasoned succulents, Lindsey and Ryan airlifted off, giggling over Yung Lu's getaway. In the distance, foghorns boomed mournfully, and the fallout filtered toward them, draping the daylight in fumes. Murky and still against the backdrop, Elsinore looked like a ghost town.

As the last shopkeepers cranked their shutters closed for the day, Lindsey and Ryan headed south along Main Street. Lindsey wanted to swing by the prison to find out who was locked up, but with pitch blocking half their view, Ryan refused to risk getting stranded. Nevertheless the identity of the mysterious prisoner weighed on her mind, and something else was bothering her, something about the Blue Brigade. Suddenly it hit her.

"Dogberry's left the big-shot prisoner unguarded!" she exclaimed.

"They've got to have other guards."

"Or maybe the prisoner got away?"

"Not a chance. Zach told me they just put in extra security." Ryan dismissed the whole prisoner business with a shrug, but Lindsey couldn't let the idea go. She was determined to find out who'd been locked up.

"What do you think 'Rose pink in the clink' means?" she asked. "Maybe it's from Shakespeare."

"No, and 'Jedgar' isn't either, in case you're wondering."

"We should have asked Yung Lu. He could have told us."

"When are you going to wake up? Oldies never give straight answers. The only way we're going to find out anything around here is by ourselves."

"You know, I sometimes think we're looking at things all wrong," she said thoughtfully.

"Could be. We sure don't have much evidence. All we know is that volcano is causing an awful lot of trouble, and we're spending half our time grounded. Mayor-Shall-Rule, animal emergencies, black-outs – we're getting nowhere fast."

"You still think Shakespeare's the key?" she asked.

"Absolutely, but what good's a key if we can't figure out what it unlocks?"

"Whoever's in jail might give us a clue."

"All right. I've got the picture. It's probably just some oldie, but we'll check it out. I'll see if the old face-bracer will let me use the blimp again."

Ryan got Lindsey home before the haze snuffed out Elsinore. He even managed to slip into his room just before his Uncle Jerry marched by hollering, "How sharper than a serpent's tooth it is to have a thankless child."

*

When the fallout settled and the sky cleared, Ryan and Lindsey got off to a fast start. They rushed through their errands and blimped southward over Main Street to Elsinore Prison. As they approached, they could hear the tiglon bellowing from the wilds of Arden Forest. Assistant Constable Dull, clad from head to toe in chain mail, was orchestrating the hunt from behind his bullet-proof barricade on the prison sunroof.

He blew his whistle. "Where are you going?"

"We want to talk to Chief Constable Dogberry," yelled Ryan, cupping his mouth so the sound would carry over the racket.

"Does Dogberry want to see you?" Dull asked suspiciously.

"It's official business," said Ryan.

"Top secret," added Lindsey with a haughty air that her aunt would have appreciated.

"Then stay way above the tree tops. That tiglon's an ornery beast."

Ryan landed the blimp on the far end of the roof, jumped out, and tapped on the garret door.

"Who's there?" came a drowsy voice.

"Ryan Mandher. You know me. I'm here with Lindsey O'Neill."

"O'Neill?"

"Yes."

The door cracked ajar, and Dogberry emerged, shaking his jowls. Lindsey noticed a dry egg noodle still imbedded in the shag.

"You're Mr. Dogberry?" said she, relieved that he didn't seem to recognize her.

"Chief Constable Dogberry," he corrected. He patted his badge. "I am a wise fellow, and, which is more, an officer … and one that knows the law."

"Pleased to meet you," said Lindsey, growing confused. She had no idea who to ask for. "We'd like to talk to the ... uh ... the prisoner."

Dogberry took her request in stride. "She won't talk. She's afraid of being voice-printed. We've got her in isolation."

"Can we see her?"

"*You* can, but *he* can't." Dogberry nudged Ryan.

"Why can't Ryan?" she asked.

"He isn't a blood relative."

My aunt's in jail, thought Lindsey, too shocked to speak.

"What are the charges against her?" asked Ryan.

"Carrying an unregistered gun. She's got an arrest record longer than Yung Lu's pigtail."

Ryan waited on the roof while Dogberry escorted Lindsey to the women's ward. They passed a dozen empty cells, all of which were painted bubble-gum pink with candy-cane-striped bars. It seemed as if the interior decorators were pretty sure who the jailbirds would be.

"I'll give you ten minutes," growled Dogberry, leaving her at the last cell.

Lindsey peered through the bars. A lady of medium height with loose-flowing red hair turned around to face her. She was strikingly pretty, and she didn't look any older than Tiffany. And she was almost Lindsey's double.

"Aunt Marie!" gasped Lindsey, her knees buckling under her.

The red-haired inmate thrust her arms through the bars, drew Lindsey toward her, and planted a sloppy kiss on her forehead.

"You're my *other* Aunt Marie!"

The newly discovered aunt pointed to her name tag. It read "Marie Rosette O'Neill, Pink Party President."

"I'm Lindsey – I mean, I'm Rosalind — Bill's daughter. You know, your nephew in San Diego, William Bryson O'Neill."

She embraced Lindsey again, her eyes brimming with tears.

"How come you're here? Can I get you out?"

Aunt Marie Rosette silently pointed to the wall clock. She seemed to be indicating the hour of twelve.

"Midnight?"

The aunt kept pointing at the clock and shaking her head.

"Noon?"

She nodded and began pantomiming as if playing charades. She prompted Lindsey with hand signals and gestures, and Lindsey started fast-fire guesswork.

"Dogberry sneezes, no, snoozes, Dogberry takes cat-nip, no, he cat-naps all day, and at noon the deadhead, no, the dummy, the flying dumbot, Dull, Dull at noon flies away, Dull swallows, no, Dull eats, he eats lunch – I've got it! Dogberry always takes a nap at noon when Dull goes home for lunch."

The aunt applauded.

"I'll be back the first day I can," promised Lindsey, "at noontime, and we'll find a way to spring you out of here."

Marie Rosette flung her arms toward the ceiling as if to say, "Heaven be praised!"

"Your ten minutes are up," barked Dogberry. He took Lindsey back to the sunroof.

The moment the blimp was aloft, Lindsey started spilling her story. She talked so hard and so fast that Ryan's ears did a drum roll.

Chapter Thirteen

BARDOLATRY

A meeting of the Rangers was long overdue, and Ryan rounded them up. They begged and borrowed blimps and hustled over to McSolid's Food Factory, better known as Maxi's, the official clubhouse – and the surest place in town to avoid running into oldies.

With the blackout still dragging on, most of the tastiest items were unavailable and crossed off the menu. The restaurant had made the mistake of purchasing a generator from Fleecer, and even the refrigerator was on the fritz. A droopy-eyed dumbot lolled by the cash register dispensing warm lemonade and sandwiches.

Ryan called the meeting to order, collected the question lists, and introduced Rhett and Oscar to the other Rangers.

"Where are Richie and Chip?" he asked.

"Those geeks? Too durn busy playing keep-away from City Hall," griped Rhett. "'Spect *me* to bring 'em the news."

"You're from Dixie?" said Cerise, her gaze lingering on Rhett. He looked quite dapper, and Lindsey caught a spark of interest between him and Cerise.

"Chattanooga, sure 'nuf, Ma'am," said he, his mouth widening into an easy grin.

"Before we start analyzing the questions, I want to ask Cerise what she found out about the church she goes to." Ryan turned to her. "Got anything to report?"

"My Great Granny Ellis wrote down the name for me." She dug into her tote bag, pulled out a piece of paper, and read, "The Church of Saint William the Divine upon Avon."

"What kind of religion is it?" asked Lindsey.

Cerise studied her notes. "It's called Bar … Bardo … Bardolatry."

"Never heard of it," said Zach.

"It means they worship William Shakespeare." Ryan positively glowed. "I knew I was right."

"You're a genius!" exclaimed Lindsey.

"Some are born great," said Ryan.

Cerise looked so bewildered that Lindsey dissected the term for her. "The word 'bard' means poet, and people call Shakespeare 'the Bard,' so Bardolatry is Shakespeare worship."

"Cerise," said Ryan, "think hard. Do people of all colors go there? Pinks, Whites, and Blues?"

"Yes!"

"Which confirms my hypothesis. That's a big help. Now let's take the questions." Ryan took Cerise's list and read aloud the only question on it, "How come there are so many blackouts?"

"Maybe the volcano is causing them," said Zach lamely.

"There is no volcano," piped in Oscar and Rhett, and the rest of the Rangers gaped in disbelief.

"You guys been brainwashed?" asked Jack, gearing himself up to pick on the two newcomers.

"I reckon I know what I'm talkin' about, li'l boy," said Rhett dismissively, "and I'm purdy sure it's jedgarmade."

"We can prove it conclusively." Oscar looked around for a monitor. "We've got it on a disk."

"No power here. Show 'em the stills," drawled Rhett.

Oscar withdrew a stack of photos from his briefcase and spread them around the table. Bathed in different lights, the mountain seemed to change shape and coloration as if it could alter its aspect at will.

"Notice anything suspicious?" asked Oscar. He flipped through the pictures and pointed to the shots he'd taken just before the fireball caused the tidal waves.

The Rangers crowded around to look. Even though none of them had ever laid eyes on a real volcano, they promptly agreed that Mount Cinderella didn't in the least bit resemble one.

Lindsey studied the mountain carefully. The surface seemed artificially smooth and glossy like overcooked pie crust. Its unusual appearance couldn't be explained by erosion or any other natural causes she could think of. Was it really jedgarmade?

When the Rangers finished viewing the pictures, Oscar gave a briefing. He told them that he and Rhett had been coming to Pensioners' Paradise every summer, and Mount Cinderella always had been a normal-looking mountain covered with trees, waterfalls, and wildlife. In those days the Inferno was called Eden Isle, and people used to ferry back and forth regularly. It was a great place to go swimming or mountain climbing – nothing dangerous about it.

Last summer when Rhett and Oscar were flying home together, they passed Eden Isle and noticed cargo planes landing all over it. That seemed odd because the island was uninhabited, but neither of them thought much about it until they returned to Pensioners' Paradise a few weeks ago and saw that the island had undergone a radical transformation. Mount Cinderella had changed from a dewy green mountain into a smoldering cinder block. Eden Isle had become the Inferno.

Lindsey couldn't believe her ears. Who'd want to rig up such a monstrosity? She wondered if an enemy power could be involved.

Rhett picked out a blow-up of the summit and said, "Take a close look at this one."

They speechlessly passed the photo around for a second viewing. No doubt about it, the summit was very strange. And disconcerting. A pattern of dark grooves or ridges wound up to top, turning the mouth of the crater into a scowl. Something about it reminded Lindsey of the nozzle on a garden hose.

"It's like some kind of diabolical weapon," observed Ryan.

"I've got a surprise for y'all," bubbled Cerise, opening a package. "I silk-screened T-shirts so the Rangers can all wear uniforms."

"Uniforms? That's brilliant! Just what a spy team needs," said Jack, dripping with sarcasm. "Nice and noticeable. When I'm head of the Secret Service, I'll make sure all the spies wear identical uniforms."

Cerise looked so crestfallen that Lindsey felt sorry for her. "That was really thoughtful of you, Cerise," she said, taking a T-shirt and trying it on over her clothes. "Awesome."

The shirts were awesome indeed – spanking white with one bright blue sleeve and one bright pink sleeve and a geometric motif over the heart, which turned out to be block letters that spelled "Ryan's Rangers."

"Thanks a lot, Cerise," said Ryan, and Lindsey could tell he was really pleased.

"I made nine of them – one for everybody, even the two geeks who didn't show up," fluttered Cerise.

"Mighty kind of you," said Rhett, rewarding Cerise with a smile so powerful that it hit a raw nerve with Zach, who hastily switched his seat to get closer to her.

Ryan took the floor again. "These photos are mind-boggling. What do you think it is?"

"Whatever the doggone thing is, it's got first-strike capacity," said Rhett.

Oscar held two photos side by side for comparison. "Look at this. The nozzle swivels 360° and can alter its size and shape before aiming. The sides of the mountain expand and contract like elastic. The amount of compression determines the force of the thrust –"

"You're right!" broke in Jack. "It's a perfect killing machine. Maybe we've discovered a military secret."

"Just a thought," said Lindsey, "but we've all been assuming that the oldies were lying or just plain mental when they said there was no volcano. And now it turns out they were right all along."

"Good point," said Ryan, arguing the flip side, "but if it looks like a volcano and acts like a volcano…."

Lindsey couldn't resist adding, "Your geology book says there aren't any volcanoes around here."

Ryan smiled wanly. "Books can be wrong. You gotta cross reference."

Oscar was getting so excited that his eyeglasses started fogging up. He wiped them on his sleeve. "It's worse than a volcano," he said breathlessly. "It's artificial intelligence. Maybe aliens. Anything that can create colossal weapons of mass destruction –"

"I don't wanna get killed," said Zach. He looked to the girls for sympathy and got none. Rhett gave him a friendly pat on the back and burst out laughing.

"Boy," he told Zach, "you're sweatin' like a flounder at a fish fry."

"The oldies are out to get us!" cried Jack.

Cerise shook her head. "My Great Granny Ellis would never hurt me. She's real sweet. And she's real nice. And she helps me take care of my Birdie.

"I agree," said Lindsey. "My Aunt Marie Celeste is a pain, but there's no way she wants us to get killed. And I don't think she tells lies either."

"The oldies might not intentionally want to hurt us," conceded Ryan, "but that mountain could wipe us out while they're arguing about leash laws. The bottom line is we can either hang around hoping we don't get blown to kingdom come, or we can take collective action. Who wants to explore the Inferno?"

He shot Lindsey a look, and she sucked in her breath so sharply she started coughing. Luckily, Oscar stepped in.

"Rhett and I already tried that," he said, "but there's something running interference – some kind of ultra-post-modern technology deflects the engines. We circled the whole island by blimp but couldn't get past the coral reef. The robots kept stalling out. It's like there's an invisible barrier that separates the Inferno from the other islands on Pensioners' Paradise."

"It isn't part of Paradise," said Cerise. "Inferno isn't part of Paradise."

The Bond brothers swapped pitying glances.

"Not so fast, guys. Maybe she's got something. Geographically it looks like it belongs to this archipelago, but geologically, it doesn't. Elsinore and the other islands have nothing but low hills, but Mount Cinderella might very well be volcanic in origin. Any more comments?" asked Ryan. He picked up Zach's question list and read the first entry, "What's a Jedgar?"

Everyone was interested in what Rhett and Oscar had to say, but Jack was antsy for the limelight. He stood up and announced that he'd seen the Jedgar with his very own eyes.

His startling news caused a sensation. With everybody's attention on him, Jack launched into a long-winded story about how he'd been surveying the Inferno day and night with his field glasses. He claimed that just as it was getting dark, he'd picked out a hulking creature near the base of Mount Cinderella. The thing looked like King Kong only it wasn't moving, just standing there like a humungous statue.

The Rangers wanted to know where the thing was so that they could take a look, and he explained that unfortunately it was gone. Whatever it was had disappeared the next morning. But he was positive it was the Jedgar. When they asked if he'd taken any pictures, the wannabe spy was forced to admit that his camera got jammed – somebody must have sabotaged the program.

Amid widespread ridicule, Jack's credibility was shot.

"I swear it's true!" he insisted, but nobody believed him.

Ryan rubbed his forehead as if trying to erase his worries. "There's got to be a way to get past the coral reef. Are there any signs of life on the Inferno?"

"We haven't found any, but we suspect that all the activity is located beneath the surface," said Oscar.

"I bet that invisible barrier is radioactive," said Zach nervously.

The generator in the corner started shaking as if trying to jumpstart itself into gear, and the electricity blinked on. The TV sprang to life, the air conditioner spat hot air, the dumbot at the cash register tooted excitedly, and the computer began to boot up. Lindsey dived for the mouse.

The background noise acted like a signal to start talking, and the meeting disintegrated. Ryan held up his hand for silence.

"Lindsey," whispered Zach loudly enough for Cerise to hear, "wanna go out with me this afternoon?"

"No." She punched in her password and logged on.

"Aw, come on, Lindsey," he said. "You're not ticked off at me, are you?"

"Leave me alone."

EEEEEEEEEEEEeeeeeeeee... keened the generator. The electricity died, and the image on the computer screen dissolved to a pinpoint. Lindsey was seriously tempted to put her fist through it.

Ryan was still doing his best to bring the meeting to order. "Come on, guys, would you all stop gabbing," he said. "I'm making plans to go to Mount Cinderella, and I want to know who's coming with me."

"HAR, HAR. Listen to the big hero," said Jack. "Be sure to tell us when you're going so I can watch the big meltdown. Can't wait to see you turn into a human you-know-what."

"You'd better shut up," hissed Ryan.

"A radioactive you-know-what," said Jack.

"I told you to shut up — unless you want to use your big mouth to volunteer."

The Jackerman preferred to shut up, so Ryan said, "I'm setting up a task force, Mission Mount Cinderella, any volunteers?"

Nobody answered, but Oscar whispered something to Rhett who gave him the thumbs up sign. Lindsey couldn't hear what was said, but she figured they were up to something.

"Ryan, I don't want y'all to melt down," said Cerise.

"Think it over and let me know," said Ryan. He skimmed over the remaining questions. "Not much here we can't table. Let's leave the rest for the next meeting. Lindsey and I've got an appointment at noon, so if there's nothing urgent...."

"I've got an urgent question," said Oscar. "Can ostriches swim?"

The Bond brothers hooted.

"I'm serious," protested Oscar. "Richie wants to dig a moat around K⁴CC, but first we've got to make sure Sherman can't swim."

"Durn bird's drivin' him crackers," added Rhett.

"We'll try to find out," said Ryan, calling for a motion to adjourn.

He felt the meeting had gone fairly well. He eyed the Rangers appreciatively. They all looked pretty sharp in their brand new T-shirts.

*

Hardly daring to breathe, Ryan and Lindsey pulled onto the sunroof of Elsinore Prison where Chief Constable Dogberry, who wasn't up for immediate re-election, was reclining on a lawn chair snoring into his ten-gallon hat. Lindsey tiptoed past him and tried the door. It was fastened with a heavy, iron padlock.

"ZZZZZZZ," went Dogberry.

"How are we going to get in?" whispered Ryan. He jiggled the padlock.

"Maybe we can pick it open," she said. "You don't have a pen, do you?"

"No, but I always carry a coat hanger with me."

"Very funny," she said. "Let's check his pockets."

As if he could sense her talking about him, Dogberry rotated his head and gave off a series of snorts. Lindsey froze, afraid he'd blow the hat off his face and see her. When his breathing grew rhythmic, she leaned over and inspected his badge. The pin on the back would make a handy tool if only she could unfasten it. Careful not to wake him, she slipped her fingers under his lapel and felt for the hook.

"What are you doing?" asked Ryan.

"Here!" she whispered, triumphantly flashing the badge. "We're in business."

Picking a padlock was a lot more difficult than Lindsey had anticipated. Even though the pin fit perfectly into the keyhole, it didn't work. She turned it back and forth, poked it in and out, shook it, and tugged, but nothing happened. Frustrated, she gave the padlock a kick. It made a hard clank against the door but didn't open.

"Brilliant," said Ryan.

"There's got to be a way," she murmured.

"With no key?"

"You're the one who keeps saying that Shakespeare is the key. Think of something!"

"You want me to recite Shakespeare?" he grumbled heading back to the blimp. "Romeo, Romeo, wherefore art thou Romeo?"

"Ryan!" she called in a hoarse whisper, "Come back. The padlock wiggled."

He did a double-take. "You're serious?"

"I'm telling you it wiggled. All by itself. Watch: Romeo,

Romeo, wherefore art thou Romeo?" she said. The padlock wiggled again. "See?"

"It wiggles, but it doesn't open."

"We're probably using the wrong lines. How about...Open Sesame?"

"That isn't Shakespeare." Ryan's photographic memory sifted through tens of thousands of stored lines. "I've got it!" he exclaimed, and he began reciting into the keyhole:

> The raging rocks
> And shivering shocks
> Shall break the locks
> Of prison gates ...

The padlock burst apart, and the door swung ajar. One by one every lock in the prison clicked open.

"Awesome!" said Lindsey.

The inmates below let off jubilant squeals. In a fever to escape, they sprang from their bunks and pushed their way into the corridors, jamming the exits. Somebody yelled, "Windows!" Slinging their pets over their shoulders, the footloose oldies leaped out the windows, raced across the yard, scaled the picket fence, and vanished into Arden Forest.

"ZZZZZZ," went Dogberry, pulling the flaps of his hat down over his ears to block out the disturbance.

Lindsey whispered to Ryan, "Let's get to my aunt before we lose her."

By the time they reached her wing, she was already skipping toward them with a devil-may-care gleam in her eye and a bottle of Montezuma water in her hand. They raced up to the sunroof and within moments were safely airborne and floating away from Elsinore Prison.

Lindsey suddenly realized that she was still holding Dogberry's badge. With a lighthearted laugh, she pitched it overboard.

"Can you speak to us now, Aunt Marie Rosette?" she asked.

"Sure. And call me Rosie. Who's your friend?"

"Ryan Mandher, the mayor's nephew."

"Poor kid," laughed Rosie. "How are your teeth?"

Ryan made a goofy face.

"Hey, land the blimp a sec. I gotta to pick up my cat," said Rosie. "Here, Kitsy, Kitsy. Come on, Kitsy."

Ryan gave the command to lower the blimp.

"You aren't afraid of getting arrested again?" asked Lindsey.

"No way. I'm free as a bird. We got laws against double jeopardy, so I can't get pinched twice for the same crime."

"I don't think double jeopardy works that way," said Ryan. "You're an escaped convict."

"I got framed – a plot to keep me under wraps till after the elections."

"That's so dishonest!" said Lindsey.

"Dirty politics. It's part of the system. But don't worry, I'll get even. I'm gonna vote twice in the next election." Rosie smiled complacently. "Wanna hear a poem? I just wrote a new one. It's like a song flung up to heaven. And it rhymes too."

"Mr. Dogberry said you were carrying an unregistered gun," said Lindsey.

"Phooey on the Blues. They're all jealous 'cuz I'm poet laureate in Elsinore. You know the worst thing about jail? Everybody's gotta drink the same water! No individualized formulas!"

"What about the GUN?" asked Lindsey.

"And I'm lobbyin' to get the airport named Tisquantum International. In Pink-think, Tisquantum was the very first American to ever meet the Bard."

"She must mean Squanto," explained Ryan, delving into his memory box. "You know, the Native American who helped the Pilgrims survive. They called him Squanto, but his real name was Tisquantum. He was from Patuxet village in Massachusetts where the Mayflower landed in 1620. But years before that, when Shakespeare was still alive, Squanto got kidnapped by a British sea captain and wound up in London where he learned English and performed in theaters before getting home again. That means Shakespeare and Squanto could have met when –"

"ROSIE, DO YOU HAVE A GUN?"

"Get a load of it." Rosie drew a squirt-gun from her hand-embroidered holster, and she sprayed them with rose-water. "I always carry perfume with me. It's genuine imported, and I make it myself."

Lindsey tried to figure out what that meant while her aunt kept on calling, "Kitsy!"

Out of a thicket leaped the six-hundred-pound tiglon.

"HELLLLLLLP!" screamed Lindsey.

"Get the blimp out of here!" Ryan snapped his fingers so hard that he nearly set off sparks.

"I want my cat!"

The tiglon lifted itself onto its hind legs and delivered a heart-rending, "GRRRUUUUGGH."

"You mean *that!*" Ryan pointed at the tiglon.

"It's okay, Kitsy. Mama's here to take care of you." Rosie turned to Ryan, and she stamped her foot. ""Let him in or I'm gettin' out!"

"You want to put *that* animal into *this* blimp?" Lindsey's face turned purple.

"You've been livin' in the Blue Zone too long. Next you'll be scared of your own shadow," huffed Rosie.

Lindsey's mind drifted back to her first evening in Elsinore when shadows along Main Street almost spooked her out of her skin. It occurred to her that maybe she really did have an over-active imagination. But on second thought, maybe Rosie was criminally insane. The smart thing to do was to let her out of the blimp. She looked as if she could fend for herself.

"You mean the tiglon isn't dangerous?" asked Ryan. "It looks pretty belligerent to me."

"Belligerent! My Kitsy isn't belligerent! Don't you dare call him belligerent!" cried Rosie. She turned to Lindsey and de-manded, "What does belligerent mean?"

"Fighting mad?"

"Kitsy isn't fighting mad. He's got a terrible toothache, poor baby." She fixed her eye on Ryan. "And *your* uncle refuses to treat him. Probably scared of getting another little scar or two."

The tiglon snarled menacingly and scratched the air with its paws.

"You're perfectly sure it won't hurt us?" ventured Ryan.

"Of course. Now let him aboard or I'm gettin' out and takin' him home by my lonesome. I got my skateboard parked outside the prison."

Ryan and Lindsey swapped question marks.

"Everything's weird here in Paradise, but if it's okay with you...."

Lindsey gulped away the lump in her throat and nodded.

Down went the blimp, in came the tiglon. Rangers, cat, and aunt flew off to the Pink Zone. Ryan and Lindsey crouched at one end while Rosie and Kitsy cuddled at the other.

*

"You smell funny, Lindsey," said Marie Celeste, pressing a lace handkerchief to her nose, "like rose-water."

"Rose-water," said Miss Prymm.

Lindsey held out a bulging satchel. "I've brought you the new flyers."

"Let me check them." She pulled one out, held it under a lamp, and appraised the montage. "Better, much better. Can't see those crooked teeth at all. The Blue Party will be pleased that the mayor looks honest."

"Looks honest," said Miss Prymm.

"Lindsey, your father phoned while you were out, and he mentioned something about a little dog," said Marie Celeste.

To her horror, Lindsey remembered that she still hadn't answered him about the puppy. "I'll call him right back."

"Not now. I'm waiting for an important phone call."

"But –"

Up went the eyebrows. "Lesson seven!"

"Never contradict the leader of a political party," said Lindsey through her teeth.

"Correct. Chief Constable Dogberry has just informed me that the tiglon is back in the Pink Zone, so the animal emergency is officially over. Stout-hearted man. He and Assistant Constable Dull are to be awarded laurel wreaths for bravery beyond the call of duty. The Mandhers, Miss Prymm, and I will be officiating at the coronation ceremony this afternoon," said the aunt. "Then we're meeting to organize the next political caucus. Sunday is only a few days off."

"Few days off," said Miss Prymm.

"What are you standing there for, Lindsey? Go upstairs and douse yourself with deodorizing disinfectant and get rid of that dreadful odor. It's most unbecoming for a young lady to smell bad. That's lesson number ten."

Chapter Fourteen

GORILLA WARFARE

Lindsey heard Ryan's voice. She wrapped a towel around her soaking hair and tossed on a bathrobe before grabbing her walkie-talkie. It struck her that mini-screens could sometimes be a drag.

"Got any volunteers for Mission Mount Cinderella?" she asked.

"Nothing definite. The kids are pretty nervous."

"Oh," she whispered. She was nervous about it too. She hadn't made up her mind yet and was grateful he wasn't pressuring her.

"Anyhow, that's not what I'm calling about," said he. "There's something going on in Arden Forest."

"What?"

"I don't know exactly. Everybody's being really mysterious. See, when we were dropping off Rosie, Zach was over here laying his Mr. Charming act on Aunt Sally. She thinks he's the greatest thing since Montezuma water got discovered."

"What's that got to do with Arden or anything else?"

"I think she's playing Cupid or something like that. She asked me to make sure you took a walk in Arden Forest."

"What for? So I can run into Zach? No thanks."

"He won't be there."

"How do you know?"

"Cerise says he goes to choir practice with her every afternoon."

"He does, does he?" Her blood temperature started mounting. "What am I supposed to see if Zach isn't there?"

"Beats me. But I'm gonna check it out."

"All right, I'm coming too. But I've got to clear it with Rosie. She wants me to visit. Says it's about time we got to know each other...."

"I'm not allowed to use the blimp anymore."

"Oh, no!"

"Stupid tiglon scratched up the interior. Old Brace the Face thinks I did it. Wants me to pay for the reupholstering out of my allowance."

"We don't need to fly; Mayor-Shall-Rule's been suspended," said she. "We can bike over."

"Too hilly. Let's take a rickshaw."

"I'll pick you up in an hour."

*

The woods were lovely, dark and deep. Ryan and Lindsey left the rickshaw at the edge of Arden Forest and made their way on foot. A thousand fragrant posies marked their path – daisies pied and violets blue and lady-smocks all silver-white. Ryan took over the task of orienteering while Lindsey picked wildflowers for her Aunt Rosie.

"What kind of clues are we looking for?" said Lindsey as they came to the edge of a clearing.

"Try to find stuff with a Shakespeare connection."

"Yeah, sure, maybe we'll run into Romeo –"

"EEEEeeeeaaaaiiii!" A chilling cry brought them to a stand-still.

"What was that?"

"Shhh!"

Ryan and Lindsey crouched behind a shrub. A walking shadow, then another, and then a third came slithering through the foliage. Dressed like witches in black robes and pointed hats, three hags burst into the clearing, cackling like bells jangled out of tune and harsh.

First witch:

> When shall we three meet again?
> In thunder, lightning, or in rain?

Second witch:

> When the hurly-burly's done,
> When the battle's lost and won.

Third witch:

> That will be ere the set of sun.

The three witches put their heads together and cried:

> Fair is foul, and foul is fair,
> Hover through the fog and filthy air.

With a final shriek, they danced off.

"So the oldies are rehearsing *Macbeth*!" laughed Ryan, releasing tension.

"For the Shakespeare festival –"

"Uh-huh. Fair is foul, and foul is fair!"

"*That's* what your aunt wanted us to see? A dress rehearsal? Give me a break!" She tossed her head and sauntered away.

"Where are you going?"

"To finish the bouquet," she said. "Aunt Rosie loves wildflowers."

Nevertheless Ryan's question got her thinking how near they were to Dogberry's Retreat where Zach lived. She wondered what Zach had told Mrs. Mandher. Maybe he'd finally come to his senses and dumped Cerise. It occurred to her that with any luck, she might run into Romeo after all!

"Don't the Bond brothers live somewhere around here?" she asked, and Ryan pointed toward the eaves of a fortress, visible through the treetops.

From then on, Lindsey selected only the wildflowers that took them along the path to Dogberry's Retreat – Zach's house. Every so often, she'd cast her eyes around as if she were still on the lookout for clues, but her thoughts were on Zachary Bond.

When she paused to examine a yellow wagtail's nest in the crook of a greenwood tree, she noted something odd.

"Ryan, look at this. There's a poem tacked to the tree.

"Wait till I tie my sneaker."

Neither he nor Lindsey saw the gorilla poised to pounce from a low-lying branch, but the gorilla saw them. It glared down at Lindsey.

"It's a love poem and my name's on it." She felt a blush rising. "My real name – Rosalind."

"Read it aloud," he said. And she read:

> From the east to western Ind
> No jewel is like Rosalind.
> Her worth being mounted on the wind
> Through all the world bears Rosalind ...

"GRRAAAAAAHHH!" bellowed the gorilla, rolling back its lips and baring its teeth. As if possessed by demons, it clapped its ears, hopped up and down on one foot, and let off a weaker but equally tortured, "Grraaaaaahhh!"

"HELLLLLP!" hollered Lindsey.

In the scramble to escape, she stumbled over her feet and bumped headlong into Ryan just as the gorilla quivered, contorted, and caved in. It plummeted through a bed of leaves and with an ear-splitting crash landed flat on its back in the exact spot she'd been reading the poem.

"Gorilla!" she gasped.

"It doesn't look like it'll get up again too soon," Ryan said, appraising the situation from a safe distance before cautiously stepping toward it. The gorilla appeared to be in critical condition, mewling and spewing its final moments.

"Ryan," she said shakily. "It's got a tail! Gorillas don't have tails!"

The thick prehensile tail was snaking toward her, arching upward like a cobra ready to strike. Ryan pulled her out of range, and the tail recoiled.

They gaped at the ape as it lay, eyes wide open, dumbly staring back. Lindsey moved aside, and the eyes followed her.

"I hate to say this, but I think it was stalking you," said Ryan.

"Huh?"

"Come here. Now try walking around it, but don't get too close."

She slowly circled the gorilla. Its grizzly head rotated after her.

"You were the target all right."

"Then why didn't it attack me? How come it just went mental and fell out of the tree? It doesn't make sense."

"Something must have stopped it."

"The poem!" exclaimed Lindsey. "It had to be the poem!"

"Shakespeare!" cried Ryan, snatching the page and glancing over the lines. "That's what did it. It can't stand to hear Shakespeare."

The gorilla scratched its nails into the soil and dug up divots of moss.

"You've got a photographic memory," said Lindsey. "Try some more!"

Ryan took a dramatic stance, aimed his finger at the creature, and recited:

> Now am I dead,
> Now am I fled,
> My soul is in the sky.
> Tongue, lose thy light;
> Moon, take thy flight.
> Now die, die, die, die, die!

He'd hardly pronounced the last word when the gorilla let loose an agonized howl. Its chest popped open, and a dozen metal coils sprang out from a control panel. The beast was heard no more.

"It's a robot!" cried Lindsey. "Why would a robot come after *me*?"

"Haven't the foggiest," said Ryan.

"Could be a freak accident?"

"No way."

They stared at each other completely stumped. Lindsey inspected the motionless hulk on the ground. It looked a lot like King Kong.

What if Jack hadn't been lying, and Ryan had just killed the Jedgar? No, she decided, that didn't add up. The Jedgar couldn't be a robot. A human being must have programmed it; otherwise the only possible explanation was extra-terrestrials.

"What are we going to do?" she asked.

He passed his hand across his brow. "First thing to do is get some Shakespeare fixed in your brain so if anything attacks again, the words come out of your mouth like a reflex response. No hesitation."

"I'll pick something really easy to memorize."

Ryan pulled out his walkie-talkie and called K⁴CC. After a short wait, he heard Oscar's tinselly voice.

"Just ran into a bad problem," said Ryan. "A robot that looks like a gorilla tried to attack Lindsey."

"Yo! What's the story?"

"She's pretty shaky, but she's fine. The ape is dead."

"Where are you?" said Oscar.

"Arden Forest near Dogberry's Retreat."

"Need help?"

"We could use a geek to figure out the program in its black box. Can Richie or Chip do that?"

"No sweat," said Oscar.

"And tell the guys they've all gotta memorize some Shakespeare. Fast."

"Huh?"

"I'll explain later."

"Listen, Ryan, stay where you are and don't touch anything. Cordon off the area so nothing can contaminate the evidence. Rhett and I'll be right over to shoot pictures of the crime scene. Then we'll take the ape back to the lab for testing."

"Just like police work," said Ryan.

He looked over his shoulder to see what Lindsey was up to only to find her bending over the beast, bestrewing the body with blossoms.

*

Tea-time at Rosie's meant lots of goodies for chewsy guests – pistachio nuts, popcorn, and coffee toffee. Except for Lindsey, the guests of the day were all four-legged, and the hostess sat Indian-style on the deck of her tree house, tossing crumbs to a family of hamsters. Kitsy rested his head on Rosie's lap, and she tickled his chin until he purred.

"He's feelin' fine and dandy," said Rosie. "I fixed his tooth all by my lonesome. But I'm gonna report that quack Jerry Mandher to the Prevention of Cruelty to Pets Association."

Lindsey took in the view of Walden Pond. Lush tropical vegetation lined the shore, and lily pads studded the sun-drenched waters. A little old man in a little old canoe paddled out to serenade his little old sweetheart. The sound of his ukulele wafted over the waves and slowly faded. Rosie hummed throatily to herself, her eyes growing misty as if she'd already forgotten that Lindsey was there.

"If music be the food of love, play on," she whispered to nobody in particular. As if on cue, the music started up again. Rosie wrapped her arms around the tiglon and gently rocked back and forth. She seemed to be cradling a world of warm feelings, soft as the whisper of a summer sea.

"It's so good to be home! Do you like it here, Lindsey? Can you feel the enchantment?"

Lindsey smiled appreciatively. Under a blanket of blue air, a filigree of treetops shaded the house. Framed in greenery, the sparsely furnished rooms were pure Disney in style. Like a theme park, one game area opened into another, enticing her to explore the next.

"It's my dream house," smiled Rosie. "Odorous at sunrise a garden of beautiful flowers."

"Rosie!" called a voice from below. They looked out and saw an old woman in a jogging suit.

Rosie waved to her. "Hiya, Juanita, what's up?"

"Bunch of us girls going to Oprah's new gym tonight. She's offering a big promo. Free aerobics classes for seniors. Want to come?"

"Could I use a workout or what!"

"Glad you're out of jail, kiddo. Jog on, jog on, the footpath way," chuckled old Juanita Shringapur. She did two brisk knee-bends and trotted off.

"Lindsey, I feel like catchin' up on all the fun I'm missin'. Wanna go to the playground?" said Rosie. "It's just down the lane. Whaddabout the amusement park? You like roller coasters, doncha?"

"Sure do," grinned Lindsey, thinking to herself that nothing seemed to faze the Pinks.

Then it struck her that even if everything appeared to be different on this side of Paradise, the danger remained unchecked. She envisioned the black volcano exploding, destroying everything in its path, pouring rivers of red and yellow lava into a sea of flames. The thought sobered her.

"I just love roller coasters," said Rosie. "And we can have a picnic barbecue tomorrow. Invite all your friends."

Lindsey was growing tired of the chit-chat. Determined to get some answers, she began to move the conversation in the direction of the Jedgar.

"You know, Rosie, I've been meaning to ask you a couple of questions. Like … um … can you train any kind of animal?"

"Sure can."

"What about an ostrich?"

"You mean Sherman? Whadda birdbrain," she laughed. "He's been playin' hooky since I got tossed in the clink."

"He could use a few more lessons. Maybe a personal trainer," said Lindsey. She crossed her fingers tightly and went for the J-word. "Rosie, I want you to tell me about the Jedgar."

The playfulness drained out of Rosie. She looked as if she'd been slapped. A fat tear came to her eye and trickled down her cheek.

"You used that *word*."

"I'm sorry. I didn't mean to upset you." Lindsey felt terrible, but now that she'd gotten up the nerve to broach the subject, she'd hang in.

"You know about it?" asked Rosie, the tears beginning to flow.

"Not much," said Lindsey.

"It's been so long since I've heard it. Hurts me something awful."

Lindsey took Rosie's hand and stroked it gently. "You can open up to me," she said.

Rosie pulled out a tissue and noisily honked her nose. "Some things never die," she said in a faraway voice, "like the cosmic power of words – like the fate that is inked in the book of life whenever you sign your name."

Lindsey knew something about the power of words – words had given her a mother that a car crash had taken away.

Rosie sobbed and sobbed, and Lindsey wondered if she should stroke Rosie's hand some more. Some people needed lots of stroking.

Evidently Rosie wasn't one of them. Her mood suddenly shifted. She jumped up and parted the branches of her tree house, opening up an unbroken view of the Inferno. The peak of Mount Cinderella was bracketed by clouds.

"Have you ever seen such a horrible-looking place?" she fumed. "What does it look like to you?"

"Bleak and frightening," said Lindsey, unsure what she was supposed to say.

"Yes, like the one who made it that way. When I first came here, it was nice as pie. Then *he* showed up. Look at the mess he's made!"

Scarlet-faced and breathing hard, Rosie was getting so riled up that her mind started hopping around like a pogo stick. "He's to blame for all the trouble! And I get so sick and tired of wearin' these earrings, I feel like taking 'em off. But I won't, and I won't, and I won't! 'Cuz you can't out-stubborn me! The nose knows, and I swear by the Bard, I'll prove my sister wrong! Her and her fourteen minutes!"

The outburst abruptly ended, and Rosie wound down as fast as she'd wound up. A girlish blush graced her cheeks like the honey apples cozy on an overlying branch.

"I'm all tuckered out," yawned Rosie, as she stretched out her limbs. "I have no more tears to shed."

Lindsey tried to unscramble the meaning behind the chopped logic. So Marie Celeste and Marie Rosette were sisters? She'd thought they might be related like cousins. And what was the big deal about the earrings? They looked like pretty normal gold studs with a flower-bud shape. She'd have to ask, but right now she wasn't going to let anything derail the topic.

"But who *is* he?" she asked.

Rosie sighed deeply. "It started last year when he took over Eden Isle, or maybe it really began sixty years ago when I was a girl your age. A boy who was decent and sweet and good started to go wrong." She lost her temper again. "That boy turned into a monster! He's been plaguing us out of spite! Spite is a blight – that's a poem! The king of the castle is a dirty rascal, and words will never hurt me! They won't, and they won't, and they won't!"

Even though Rosie was cross-legged on the floor, she managed to stamp her foot.

"Oh, no!" she cried, "My aura is fading!" She fanned her face with a waxy leaf. "No, wait. That's better. It's coming back. Gotta keep my aura."

Lindsey sniffed the air. A delicious aroma made her nose twitch. "Are you cooking something?" she asked.

"The pizza! I'd better get it before it burns." Rosie kicked off her slippers, grabbed a branch, and swung off from tree to tree.

Lindsey was relieved to find herself alone. She needed a time-out from the mood swings. As she tried to sort things out, she began to suspect that Rosie had revealed something important, but what? Rosie was so scatterbrained it was hard to figure out what she was talking about, but at least she'd pretty much confirmed the Rangers' theory that the Jedgar was an evil madman.

Nevertheless, something about Rosie's reaction to the J-word kept preying on Lindsey's mind, something she couldn't put her finger on. It seemed to her that while the J-word upset all the oldies, Rosie's reaction was more complicated as if she felt personally injured. More puzzled than ever, Lindsey was too tired to concentrate. She set the problem aside, hoping to grapple with it later.

Clasping her hands behind her head, she leaned back and closed her eyes. She was hungry, and thoughts of pizza made her mouth water – a gigantic wedge with thick golden cheese and juicy red tomato sauce drooling over a crispy crust and slowly melting, sizzling, burning like rivers of lava hissing toward her.

"No!" she cried, rousing herself.

She sprang to her feet and looked around. The hissing sound was real. Static was coming from her receiver.

SSSSSS!

"Scared of a pizza!" she grumbled. "I'm really losing it. Before long I'll be crazier than the oldies."

"SSSSSSay, Lindsey."

"Who is it?" she asked, shaking the walkie-talkie until Ryan's face appeared.

"Lindsey, are you sitting down?"

"Spare me the theatrics."

"Oscar just phoned with the lab results. He says the gorilla-robot thing is called a gorbot. The memory box shows that it's newly-minted, only a couple of weeks old."

"It was built while we were here?"

"Uh-huh. And here's the worst part – sorry to have to tell you, but the geeks discovered a composite drawing of you in the hard disk with the command to go after you."

"No!" She sat down with a thud.

His eyes clouded with concern. "It's like somebody knew you'd arrived."

"But why *me*?"

Good question, but neither of them had an answer. They wracked their brains trying to think of a reason why Lindsey would be singled out for attack.

After a long silence, Ryan said, "You were right about why it crashed. Any kind of poetry bugs a gorbot's system, but Shakespeare destroys the disk-drive. That poem you were reading saved you."

She'd heard of the power of poetry, but the idea that words could serve as a shield … the cosmic power of words … in the beginning was the Word….

"Are you still there?" asked Ryan.

"Mmmm." The walkie-talkie had slipped through her fingers. She picked it up, pulled herself together, and saw his worried expression. "Ryan, was that the only gorbot?"

"What do you mean?"

"I mean, could there be others around?"

"No way to tell. Rhett's got some shots of creatures that look like baboons, but who knows if they're gorbots or just ordinary apes?"

"Why didn't he warn us?"

"How could he know? There are lots of weird pets and funny-looking robots and things all over the place, and nothing's ever attacked before."

"Well, one has now."

"Lindsey, did you find out anything from Rosie?" It was a challenge rather than a question.

"I'm not sure. She keeps flipping out, and I can't make heads or tails of what she says."

"I told you so. The oldies will never give us answers, and your Great Aunt Rosie –"

"Is a total flake," she said, finishing the sentence for him. Much as she liked Rosie, talking to her was rough – like opening a grab-bag of emotions.

"Face it, Lindsey, things are out of control. We've got to move into action before somebody gets killed."

She didn't need convincing. She'd already reached the conclusion that the danger was getting too close, and they might have to explore the Inferno. Even so, she didn't like the idea, and she kept turning it around in her mind, looking at it from all angles, and studying the options.

"It's pretty bad," she said, "but the oldies made sure we all knew a poem, so let's figure they want to protect us."

"Great protection! What happens if somebody panics and forgets the stupid poem?"

"Ryan, remember what you said, you know, how Shakespeare is the thing that unites the oldies? But there's another thing that unites them: they all hate the Inferno. Do you think there's a connection? I mean, where did the gorbot come from if it wasn't the Inferno? And it's like the oldies seem to know the Jedgar – at least Rosie met him a long time ago."

"Interesting."

"I've been thinking about Mission Mount Cinderella," she said, her imagination racing ahead. "It's pretty obvious the

Jedgar lives under the volcano – and it's probably one big power keg run by computers – if we can find the entrance, break in, get the geeks to reprogram the computers – and we'll need survival kits – ropes, tools, inflatable life-jackets, and stuff – and if we can get hold of some stun guns, maybe even capture the Jedgar –"

"Where are we going to get stun guns?"

"I'll think about it," she said. "The Jedgar has to be human, so we've gotta take stun guns. We'll plan everything down to the last detail, leave nothing to chance. You'd better call a Rangers' meeting."

"No more messing around," he said. "Hold on a minute, Aunt Sally wants to talk to you."

Mrs. Mandher came on the line. "Lindsey, are you sure you're okay? Ryan told me about the gorbot, and I feel just awful."

"I'm fine."

"That takes a load off my mind. Bye, now."

"Wait – I want to ask you a question," said Lindsey. "How come you wanted me to go to Arden Forest?"

"I'm such a fool, such an old, romantic fool. Everybody loves a lover, and when that adorable young Zachary poured his heart out to me, I wanted to help him. I thought that some poems with your name might make you like him."

"He copied love poems for me?"

"Not exactly." Mrs. Mandher smiled apologetically. "His handwriting is such a mess. I copied them out of my Shakespeare book and had a dumbot attach them to all the greenwood trees in the hope you'd come across a few. I didn't realize you'd run into disagreeable company."

"Disagreeable company? That ape-thing could have killed me!"

"Now, now, you're upset after all. I'd suggest you drink a nice, hot cup of chamomile tea and forget all about it."

Lindsey couldn't believe her ears. Ryan was right — even the oldies who *appeared* to be fairly normal were totally out of their gourds.

"You know where the gorbot came from?" she asked.

"I've got some ideas, but that doesn't matter now that Ryan put it to sleep. The only important thing is love. And I ought to know better than to meddle with sweethearts. You'll forgive me, won't you?"

"Sure," said Lindsey. It wasn't too hard to forgive Mrs. Mandher, but Zach was another story.

"Then all's well that ends well. Toodle-ooo, Lindsey."

Rosie showed up balancing a pizza tray on her head. "I just adore pepperoni and mushrooms," said she. "At Elsinore Prison, the only *mush* room's the kitchen. The chef's a Blue. I got so hungry for solids, I nearly bit him."

She sliced the pizza into wedges and topped them with fresh basil leaves, and they both dug in.

"Prison's a drag! They tried to snatch my perfume," pouted Rosie. She took her squirt-gun from its holster and sprinkled herself and Lindsey with a cascade of rose-water. "Perfume feels sooo yummy. It's like wearing candy!"

"Rosie, I've got to tell you, I was attacked by a gorbot yesterday."

"No," she said vacantly. "Perfume is much better than candy 'cuz it's good on the outside where everybody can enjoy it. It's like wearing a poem. I wonder if anybody ever ate a poem."

"Any idea why the gorbot attacked me?" asked Lindsey.

"Maybe if I wear two kinds of perfume like chocolate and vanilla –"

"ROSIE, do you know why the gorbot attacked me!"

"Nope," she said, helping herself to another wedge of pizza and sharing it with the tiglon. "Kitsy just loves mozzarella."

"That gorbot nearly killed me!" cried Lindsey, trying to provoke a reaction.

"What's a gorbot?"

"It's a robot that looks like a gorilla."

"We Pinks don't keep gorbots. Live animals are much better," said Rosie. "You gotta believe in life."

It occurred to Lindsey that if the gorbot was a new invention, maybe Rosie had been in jail when it was being built.

"You've never heard of a gorbot?"

Rosie shook her head. Her expression was wide-eyed and innocent.

So she really didn't know! Somehow Lindsey had taken it for granted that all the oldies knew what was going on in Elsinore, but what if they were just as confused as the kids? The idea troubled her. Even a conspiracy seemed preferable to raw ignorance.

"Ask my twin sister. She's the know-it-all," said Rosie.

"You and Marie Celeste are twins? You don't look alike." Or act alike, thought Lindsey. She wondered how long the feud between them had been going on, and she pictured a pair of newborns, one with a mop of red hair and the other with a blue head-hive, slugging it out in a crib.

"Celestie's fourteen minutes older." Rosie took a swig of her Montezuma Lite, Fizzy Formula 44, and sloshed it around her mouth before gulping it down. "Big sister act – always worryin' about who's aging gracefully and who's aging disgracefully. She's been bossin' me around since I was born."

"That, like, doesn't make sense. She's only a few minutes older."

"Her type always gets an early start."

Lindsey's walkie-talkie started vibrating. "I've been looking for you everywhere, Lindsey," scolded Marie Celeste. "What are you doing?"

"Nothing."

"Come home right this minute! Over and out."

"See," smirked Rosie. "Bossy, bossy, bossy!"

*

"UGH!" went Marie Celeste when Lindsey entered the house. She pressed her lace handkerchief to her nose.

"UGH!" went Miss Prymm.

"Didn't you shower with disinfectant? You're still reeking."

Lindsey sniffed the air and detected a soft, sweet scent of roses.

"May I, ahem, pertinaciously propose that the charming young lady try scrubbing with tomato juice and salt water," said Dr. Mandher. "It works on skunks."

"Lindsey, get a carton of tomato juice and go down to the beach. Don't come back until the smell is gone."

*

The sea was deliciously cool, and the air was balmy. Lindsey swam for a while. Then she spread her beach blanket on the sand and stretched herself out to soak up the late afternoon sun. Out of the corner of her eye, she could see the distant whales cavorting over the water. Their fluke prints spread like huge pods over the flat surface.

She was getting set to leave when Jack swaggered over and plunked himself down beside her. His sunburn had turned into splotches, and he busied himself peeling the dead skin from his shoulders.

"Hey, Carrot Head, what'll you give me if I tell you where Zach and Cerise are?" he asked cockily.

"Couldn't care less. Get off of my towel." She snatched it out from under him, and he landed in a pile of kelp.

"Learn anything about the Jedgar?" he said unfazed.

"Maybe." She switched on her portable radio to drown him out.

"When are the Rangers meeting again?" he slugged on. The Jackerman was not easy to deflate.

"I thought it was *your* business to know things."

Turning over to get him out of her line of vision, she caught sight of Cerise and Zach strolling toward her with an arm slung around each other's neck. Lindsey averted her eyes and pretended to concentrate on lathering her face with sunscreen. When Zach noticed her, he rudely dumped Cerise and bounded over. Cerise made two fists, planted them on her hips, and stared after him fuming.

Zach squatted beside Lindsey and said, "Hey, where you been?"

"From the east to western Ind." She saucily quoted the poem on the greenwood tree, but Zach gave no hint of recognition.

"Huh?" he said.

"Forget it," said Lindsey, sorry she'd ever liked such a loser. He gave her a watery smile. "You still mad at me, Lindsey?"

"Are you my boyfriend or not!" cried Cerise, storming over to confront Zach.

"Hold it," said Lindsey. "Did Ryan tell you to learn Shakespeare?"

"Yup," laughed Lover Boy. "I got better stuff to think about."

"What's that out on the water? A cyclone?" asked Jack. The ocean seemed to be rising into swells.

"Whales," said Lindsey without looking up.

Jack kept watching the swells as they rose into great crests. "Can't be whales. They're moving too fast." He pulled out his field glasses and spotted four black mounds slicing through the ocean like bulldozers plowing the navy blue water into white troughs. Sea birds shrieked and scattered out of range of the advancing jaws.

With nobody paying any attention to her, Cerise exploded, "Zachary Bond, are you going to answer me!"

Jack was so paralyzed by fright that he couldn't get his mouth to work. He pressed his fingers to his throat, but no sound came out. Tongue-tied and choking, he sputtered incoherently.

"G-g-guys, hey, g-g-guys, they're h-h-here!"

Four moby-modem hydro-jets were skimming the surface at breakneck speed. As they pulled into the shoals, their hatch doors flew open. A gigantic gorbot catapulted from the spout of each hump and charged over the waves toward shore.

Jack let off a howl, "Gorillas!"

"Gorbots!" cried Lindsey, springing to her feet. "Start reciting poetry!"

"What?" asked Cerise.

"Poetry!" screamed Lindsey. "It's the only way to stop them!"

The chase was on. The gorbots vaulted over the dunes, roaring and pounding their chests. It was a fearsome sight. The four Rangers pivoted on their heels and bolted, tossing verses into the wind.

"Little Miss Muffet sat on a tuffet," brayed the Bond brothers.

"Thirty days has September, April, June, and November," wailed Cerise.

"Over hill, over dale, through flood, through fire," hollered Lindsey.

The gorbots were catching up. Their monstrous growls closed

in. Suddenly Lindsey realized that the kids were all downwind, and their lines were being carried in the wrong direction. She turned around, squarely faced the oncoming gorbots, and shouted Shakespeare into their faces:

> Up and down, up and down,
> I will lead them up and down.
> I am feared in field and town.
> Goblin, lead them up and DOWN!

The gorbots froze as if mortally stabbed. They were almost close enough to touch her, but she stood her ground, bravely chanting her lines like a prayer.

"GRRAAAAAAHHH!" went their stricken cries.

The gorbots clutched their heads and staggered back helplessly, their growls growing faint. They toppled into the sand, and a brier patch of oscillating wires twanged from their chests. Then all was still, and nothing could be heard but the soft lapping of waves against the shore.

"What happened?" asked Jack.

"Lindsey, you're a hero!" exclaimed Cerise.

"Much ado about nothing," shrugged Lindsey, and she sauntered off to pick up her radio, her beach blanket, and her tomato juice.

*

As a zig turns into a zag, Lindsey's burst of bravura dissolved into fear. Alone in her room, afraid to fall asleep, she sat up all night with her Shakespeare book in her lap.

By morning she was burned-out and looked it. Instead of going down to breakfast, she talked Jeeves into bringing her some orange juice and toast. She'd taken only a few nibbles when she heard her aunt's stiletto heels clickety-clacking along the corridor, and she hastily hid the rest under the dish-cover.

"I smell toast!" declared Marie Celeste, wrinkling her nose in disgust. She spotted Lindsey's tray and snatched off the lid.

"Toast!" She spat out the word and fixed Jeeves with the look she reserved for deranged robots. "You've poisoned her! Get a thermometer!"

Lindsey buried her face in her pillows and moaned, "They want to kill me."

"What a notion!" Marie Celeste swabbed Lindsey's forehead with her lace handkerchief. "The poor child is delirious."

It turned out that Lindsey had a low-grade fever, and the aunt prescribed forty-eight hours of undisturbed rest. No visitors were permitted, and for two days Lindsey endured invalid treatment. Rosie sent her a get-well card with some lines she'd composed:

> Rosies are pink,
> Celesties are blue,
> Want me to smuggle
> A pizza to you?

The pizza never came. When Lindsey finally got released from sick bay, she was craving solid food so badly that she went straight to Maxi's to treat herself to a breakfast fit for a hero.

Chapter Fifteen

ENTERPRISES OF
GREAT PITH

It was lunchtime, but none of the Rangers had shown up at Maxi's, and no sign of them elsewhere in downtown Elsinore. Lindsey tried calling Ryan but couldn't get through.

Lonely as a cloud, she wandered over to Plato's Pub & Self-Service Symposium – nobody there but oldies, and no Rangers at The Coffee Toffee Taffy Tavern either, but Miss Prymm was sitting at the counter, stuffing caramels into her mouth. When she caught sight of Lindsey, she sheepishly lowered her eyes.

Lindsey moped around town until it hit her that the kids might be at Yung Lu's, and she decided to check it out. As she cut across the hypotenuse of Isosceles Square, she noticed that somebody had defaced the Shakespeare memorial by blackening one of its eyes.

"What'll you give me if I tell you who messed with the statue?" asked Jack, stepping out from behind the pedestal. He was eating a grape ice-pop, which was melting fast, and he caught the drippings with a purple tongue.

"You following me around or something?" she asked, figuring that he'd messed it up himself.

"Maybe."

"Do me a favor and get lost."

"Seen Ryan?"

"Why?" she said, all sugary. "You planning to volunteer for Mission Mount Cinderella?"

"You mean Mission Melt Down? Fat chance. He's just bluffing. Nobody in his right mind's gonna go."

Lindsey gave him a pitying look, and he backed off saying, "I'm not committing no suicide."

Noise filled the streets, a clanging and jangling like tin cans cranking out circus music, and Fleecer rattled around the corner, his tri-colored Deals on Wheels pushcart plastered with posters of vicious, man-eating fish. Fleecer's wife Imelda followed him, slapping a tambourine.

"Step right up! Come one, come all!" she shouted. "Get your tickets to Fleecer's live piranha show! Bring your honey and double your money!"

"What's that?" asked Lindsey.

"The voter bandwagon. Elections are right after the show – fireworks at midnight," said Jack, licking away at his ice-pop. "Everybody in town's gonna be there. Wanna go?"

"I've already voted."

People latched onto the procession, and the ruckus grew louder. Jack followed it with his eyes until it vanished behind City Hall.

"Big banquet at Plato's Pub tonight," he said. "All you can eat. I got tickets."

"You *bought* tickets?"

"Nah. Imelda gave them to me. She's got a real hype going. Fleecer's gonna jump into a tank full of live piranha fish. Wanna bet he survives?"

"Probably trained trout," scoffed Lindsey.

"How did you know?"

"Get lost," she said, and she stomped off to Yung Lu's.

*

Lindsey paused to read a freshly-painted sign:

YUNG LU'S RENOVATED
APOLITICAL, PATRIOTIC, OMNI-ETHNIC,
NONVIOLENT, NONSECTARIAN, NONSEXIST,
NON-POLLUTING, NON-DISCRIMINATORY,
NON-ALIGNED, EQUAL OPPORTUNITY, INOFFENSIVE,
WORLD FAMOUS, NON-GLOBAL, POST-ORGANIC
(NO ADDITIVES, NO SUBTRACTITIVES),
KOSHER AND NONKOSHER,

LEANING
(NEITHER TO THE RIGHT NOR TO THE LEFT
NOR TO THE MIDDLE)
EIFFEL TOWER OF UNIVERSALLY APPROVED
HEALTH FOOD DELICACIES

It looked as if Yung Lu was making a big effort to be politically correct.

She peeked through the kitchen window and caught sight of Fujiyama in a gondolier's hat and a boating shirt with pink, white, and blue horizontal stripes. He was skipping around the table tossing dough balls into the air.

"Yung Lu's reopening?" she asked.

"Toot, toot," went Fujiyama.

"He's already reinvented himself?"

"Toot, toot."

"He's here now?"

"Toot."

Fujiyama handed her a copy of a brand new menu, and she ran her eyes over the heading: THIS INFORMATION IS VITAL FOR YOU – PASS IT ON! A list of "viral-adjusted values" filled the rest of the page. She had no idea what a viral-adjusted value was, but she noticed that the prices had doubled. Yung Lu was returning in style.

She heard Ryan call, "Hey, Lindsey!" She looked up and saw him waving from the roof garden.

"What are you doing up there?"

"Come up and see."

She tromped up the long, winding staircase. When she reached the top, she discovered Ryan and all four K⁴CC boys huddled over pages of blueprints. It looked like Ryan had been bonding with them, and she felt a pang of jealousy.

"Where's Yung Lu?" she asked.

"Won't be back till after the elections," said Ryan. "We've commandeered the lighthouse. Gonna pay a visit to Jedgar's Inferno. We're scaling Mount Cinderella tonight."

Tonight! She felt her cheeks growing hot. So Ryan had been planning operations without bothering to even tell her. For the first time all summer, he'd cut her out of the picture, and she wondered if it was because she was a girl.

"You're serious?" she said.

"Uh-huh. Reconnaissance mission."

"What about the invisible barrier?" she asked, shifting her weight back and forth from one foot to the other as if trying to regain her center of gravity. The way he'd sprung things on her made her head spin.

"Purdy tough to fly through," drawled Rhett. "So we reckon we'll go under it."

Oscar passed her a picture of a ragged, underwater gap. "There's a big chink in the coral reef – almost five feet in diameter. We can slip through easy."

Lindsey bent over to inspect the plans and saw what looked like a doomsday mission.

"You're coming, of course?" said Ryan.

All five boys eyeballed her, and Lindsey wasn't about to let them think she felt scared.

"Count me in," she said, secretly hoping they'd all catch the mumps or whooping cough and get themselves quarantined fast. "So ... what's the plan?"

"Operation Sea-Trek," said Ryan. "Chipper invented an amphibious vehicle. A macro-mouse...."

"I call my macro-mouse the iiiEnter-Prize," noted Chip with a tad of pride. "Think different, guys!"

"The inside holds four kids," continued Ryan, "a driver – that'll be Chip, and three trekkers – that'll be you, me, and Oscar. We're going to take the submarine route to the reef, pass through the hole, land on the Inferno, and investigate."

"It might be kind of dangerous," she said, and the boys eyeballed her again.

She was on the spot, and the silence was growing unbearable.

"What I mean is ... um ... like what are we supposed to do?" But that wasn't what she wanted to say at all.

Instead, what she wanted to ask was whether they'd figured out the risk factor and what precautions they were taking. Was there a Plan B in case things went wrong? Did they have foolproof fail-safe worked out, or WHAT?

144

She wanted to see a well-thought out, carefully-organized mission that would give them a chance of survival, but she couldn't figure out how to ask. No matter what she said, she felt certain that they'd just label her a scaredy-cat.

She was getting flustered, couldn't get the words out, and she realized that she was afraid of losing face in front of the boys.

Brilliant reason to get yourself killed, she thought bitterly.

"Rhett will be up here on the roof filming us through a telescopic lens," said Ryan. "If he spots any trouble, he'll send up a flare. And Richie will provide helicopter coverage in case we need to get rescued."

"I'm taking Uncle Sammy's clipper-copter," smiled Richie.

"Chip stays with the getaway mouse while we trek. It's the only viable plan," explained Ryan. "The ground troops have got to know Shakespeare just in case."

This was too much for her to take without protest. Eyes flashing, she lashed out at Chip. "So if your mouse-mobile gets attacked, you can't defend it, and the rest of us get stranded. And it's all your fault!"

"*My* fault?"

"It wouldn't kill you to memorize some Shakespeare."

"In my spare time?" said Chip, consulting his iiiWatch.

"Then program the stupid macro-mouse to recite *Hamlet*!"

"It shouldn't be a problem," said Richie breezily. "All Chip's got to do is man the iiiEnter-Prize. If you run into trouble, swim to the coral reef, and I'll airlift you out."

"And if the barrier turns out to be radioactive, how are we supposed to get away?" she snapped.

"Unlikely. Birds and other creatures pass through, so we figure it bugs machines but doesn't harm living organisms." Richie leaned back on his elbows and grinned, and Lindsey wasn't sure how to cope with so much self-confidence.

"It's now almost thirteen hundred hours," said Chip. "Operation Sea-Trek starts at four o'clock in the morning, in precisely fifteen hours, three minutes, and sixteen seconds."

"Four o'clock in the morning!" she coughed. It was a parched little sound, impossible to mistake for whooping cough.

"Perfect timing – the oldies will all be sleeping late after the elections. We expect to go there and get back before they wake up. We've got to land on the Inferno at sunrise so we can explore without using flashlights," said Ryan.

"Oh, say," quipped Oscar, "can you see by the dawn's early light?"

Nobody bothered to groan, let alone comment. And Lindsey gnashed her teeth.

*

"Are you ready, Lindsey?" Ryan's voice rang through the walkie-talkie.

"Yes," she said.

A world of doubts swamped her. She was ready, but ready for what? She didn't dare ask. If she opened her mouth, they'd probably take off without her. She consoled herself with the thought that if the mission ran into trouble, she might be able to help.

"Open your window. We're right outside," said Ryan.

Lindsey shoved it open and saw the clipper-copter hovering overhead. A rope ladder dropped out. She worked her way onto the window ledge, grabbed the ladder with both hands, and deftly pulled herself on board. A dumbot that she recognized as Alfred turned its head to give her a lopsided grin.

"*That*'s the pilot?" she squawked.

"Not to worry," said Richie, and she felt much too disheartened to argue.

"Where's Rhett?" she asked.

"Already stationed on Yung Lu's roof."

Ryan and Oscar were wearing backpacks, and they'd brought one for her. She opened it and pawed through the survival equipment: a canteen, some bandages, a jack-knife, a chocolate bar, and an apple – but no inflatable life-jacket, no whistle, no ropes, no toolkit, no stun gun! Be prepared? The Rangers sure needed Scout training!

The roar of the engines discouraged conversation, and nobody spoke as they punctuated the darkness with an occasional yawn. The night was moonless and overcast. Ahead of them,

Elsinore Harbor stretched like tinfoil crinkling into the horizon.

"Good luck," said Richie, dropping them onto the wharf.

Chip took a remote control from his pocket and pushed a button. The iiiEnter-Prize, a mouse-shaped go-cart with flippers and a propeller tail, hustled onto the beach from its underwater mooring. Another button illuminated the headlight eyes and opened the convertible roof, revealing a row of toboggan seats. Chip lovingly patted the snout.

"Insanely great!" he shouted, dropping into the driver's pit.

Ryan, Lindsey, and Oscar piled into place behind him. The roof clicked shut, and the iiiEnter-Prize nosed into the water and skirted along the ocean floor.

"What's this macro-mouse made of?" asked Lindsey, peering through the transparent siding. Schools of silvery fish flashed past like bullets, and she felt as if she could reach out and catch them with her fingers.

"A special fiber-glass alloy called gorbot glass. Same principle as sunglasses. Outside it looks opaque so nobody can see in, but from the inside, it's transparent," explained Chip.

"Well," said she, "I was just thinking that Mount Cinderella might be made of similar material. Like from the outside it looks black, but whatever's on the inside can see us coming."

"Could be," cracked Oscar. "Let's just hope the Jedgar isn't an early riser."

The iiiEnter-Prize wiggled through the gap in the coral reef and pulled onto shore just as daybreak clawed open a sliver of light. The early morning air was chill and tingly. Chip opened the roof, and the trio of trekkers emerged wide-eyed and shivering.

Rapt in the wonder of it like pioneers on an alien planet, they surveyed the naked landscape. A thread of light twined around the base of the mountain casting a ghoulish sheen over it. Through the gloom, a dry wind was keening, and they could hear the grating roar of pebbles. In such a barren setting, nothing felt alive except the prickling of their skin.

"Take care," said Chip. He switched the iiiEnter-Prize onto "hold."

As if expecting a million movie cameras to record the landing, Oscar squared his shoulders and goose-stepped forward.

"One small step for mankind," he said.

Lindsey was in no mood to put up with a show-off. "Shut up, Oscar!" she hissed.

Ryan put his finger to his lips, and Lindsey and Oscar fell into formation. They traipsed across the beach in silence. The sand, black and grainy as peppercorns, stuck to the soles of their sneakers. Lindsey leaned over and picked up a handful. She sniffed it — odorless. She started to put a grain into her mouth, and Ryan slapped it away.

"Are you crazy?" he said. "It could be toxic waste."

As the trekkers approached the climb, the mountain no longer looked smooth and glassy. It was gutted by rockslides, and what had appeared to be sash-like grooves winding from summit to base turned out to be above-ground tubing that looked like a gutter pipe.

"Jedgarmade?" observed Lindsey.

Ryan charted the ascent with his eyes. "Might be the best way up. Let's stick to it."

They scraped the sand from their sneakers and began climbing along the gutter-pipe path. Although the surface appeared solid, it splintered under their weight, chipping loose and rolling in rivulets to the ground.

The going was steep, and it was tough making headway. They wedged their toes into tight footholds and crawled like crabs scaling a cylinder. The struggle to inch upward sapped their strength. After an hour, they'd climbed only a few hundred feet.

Lindsey was getting discouraged. "There's no entrance," she said.

"It's probably at the top," said Oscar. "Through the crater."

The further they went, the bigger the mountain seemed to grow, and Lindsey could barely manage another step. Beads of sweat trickled down her cheeks.

"How are we ever going to make it to the top?" she groaned.

Ryan's complexion was taking on the tinge of burnt molasses. He tore open his collar, rolled over, and steadied himself, squatting with his back against the slope.

"I'm suffocating. Let's catch a breather," he said.

They were all dry-mouthed, and they thirstily drained their canteens.

Oscar passed his binoculars around. In the foreground, Richie was hovering close to the coral reef. Beyond him, they could pick out the contours of Yung Lu's lighthouse jutting over the harbor like a friendly beacon reflecting the sunlight.

From their precarious perch, Elsinore looked peaceful and safe and impossibly distant. Lindsey gazed at it longingly. She wished she were there.

"We're wasting time," said Oscar, catching his second wind. He rolled back to his knees and began crawling uphill.

"Hold on." Ryan was still panting. "I hear something."

They listened. Lindsey held her breath as an almost imperceptible sound reached her ears. It was so faint that she wasn't sure she could hear it at all, but she braced herself for trouble.

"A low thudding?" she whispered.

Thumpety-thump, thumpety-thump, came the noise.

"It sounds like something's about to explode," said Ryan, cupping his ear. "Like the mountain is hollow."

Oscar said, "I can't hear anything."

"What are we *doing* here anyway? We've got no protection and no operating plan! We're sitting ducks! What are we supposed to do if we run into the Jedgar?" cried Lindsey, her anger mounting. "This place gives me the creeps!"

"You've got to be kidding. This is going to be a sensation," said Oscar. "A blockbuster! Escape to nowhere!"

"Would you guys quit squabbling and listen?" said Ryan.

Oscar pressed his ear to the mountain but still couldn't hear anything. He eased his way down to the others, lost his grip, and kept slipping. To break his fall, he kicked into the crust and set off an avalanche of pebbles.

"Woops," he giggled, sticking out an arm and latching onto Ryan. They rocked back and forth hugging each other like bears.

Oscar burst out laughing. "It's you, Ryan!"

"Me?"

"Yes, you! Hahaha! That tom-tom noise is coming from you! Sounds like a – hahaha – heart attack!"

Ryan clapped his hands to his chest and felt it heaving with a thumpety-thump, his lungs straining for air.

"Eleven-year-old boys don't have heart attacks," said Lindsey.

"I'm almost twelve."

"You're out of shape," laughed Oscar. "Do a twenty-minute workout every day. That'll tone you up fast."

"I don't have much time for sports."

"Ryan, you're sure you're all right?" asked Lindsey, and he gave her a shame-faced nod.

"Let's get moving," said Oscar. He made a brusque signal toward the lighthouse as if directing Rhett to keep on filming.

Ryan struggled to his knees, and they resumed climbing. Light and nimble as a squirrel, Oscar quickly outdistanced the others and disappeared behind the bend.

"Don't get separated!" called Ryan.

Oscar waited until they reached him and once again scrambled off. Lindsey could barely keep pace, and Ryan lagged way behind.

"I said let's not get separated," he panted. "I don't want us to lose sight of each other."

"Aw, come on, Ryan, there's nothing around here," scowled Oscar.

Lindsey was so exhausted that her legs were growing wobbly. Afraid they might start to cramp, she stopped to massage them. Rolling up her pant legs, she discovered that her knees were badly skinned but not bleeding. She began kneading her calves.

"Come on!" said Oscar.

"Wait a minute!" she snapped. She'd had her fill of him. "Can't you just stay put for one lousy minute! You think I like chasing after a little daredevil? The least you can do is stick with us!"

A shadow passed over them. The sky darkened and the wind picked up with an ominous whirring.

"What's that?" she cried, pushing the hair out of her eyes.

"Grackle birds," said Ryan, and the trekkers instinctively moved toward each other and studied the sky.

A flock of granite-gray grackles dropped out of nowhere, dipping and twisting as they flew, forming spherical patterns against the sky. Thousands filled the air like dancers performing a grotesque ritual. Traveling in great clusters, they blocked the view of Elsinore, eclipsing the daylight behind a curtain of forked wings.

Lindsey couldn't take her eyes off them. "Why are they behaving so mental?" she asked.

"Dunno," said Ryan. "I've never seen grackles do that before."

"There's something about the Inferno that causes...." said Oscar. His voice trailed off, and his eyes widened. "What a spectacle!"

Lindsey could no longer see the helicopter or the lighthouse, only the hideous birds circling in tight formations and piercing the air with their harsh, metallic cawing. All at once, they grouped and shot downward. She ducked her head. The birds swung in so close that a rush of air tickled her flesh. She could smell their foul odor.

If I ever get out of here alive, she promised herself angrily, I'm never going to let anyone talk me into doing anything this stupid again! Never, never, never, never, never!

Here she was helpless, perched on an active volcano, just because she hadn't had the nerve to challenge a bunch of little boys. For that matter, she probably wouldn't even be on Pensioners' Paradise if she'd stood up to Tiffany. Thinking back, she recalled the time she'd fallen out of a half-dead tree she'd climbed when some dumb kid had dared her.

As her life passed before her, she saw a pattern emerge: it seemed as if every time she landed in trouble, she'd allowed somebody else to push her into it. And now that she was stuck in the worst fix ever, she blamed herself for being such a wimp. Her cheeks were crimson, but not from fear.

Ryan was the first to sit up. "Anybody hurt?" he asked.

Too dazed to answer, they huddled together and stared at the birds lifting off to regroup.

"What are we going to do?" asked Oscar.

"If they come at us again, stand up and flap your arms," said Ryan. "And make a big racket."

The birds plunged. The trekkers screamed in unison and flailed their arms. Oscar wound up like a baseball pitcher, shot his canteen at the lead bird, and hit it squarely on the beak. Miraculously, the bird changed course, and the whole flock rounded the mountain and melted out of sight.

"Wow!" exclaimed Oscar, glowing with excitement. "I hope Rhett caught that."

Lindsey felt like strangling him. "You are a lunatic! Can't you think of anything but your stupid movie? What if that was some kind of warning? Birds sometimes signal disasters!"

"I hear noises," said Ryan.

"Again!" Oscar looked incredulous. "You guys are making me jittery."

"Hush." Ryan listened to the mountain. "It's not me this time."

"I hear it too – a drumming noise – and it's getting louder!" exclaimed Lindsey.

THUMP! – THUMP! – THUMP!

"The volcano's erupting!" she cried, half expecting to see torrents of lava spilling from the summit.

THUMP! – THUMP! – THUMP! – THUMP! – THUMP! The eerie beat of madness grew from the depths of the mountain and banged with increasing ferocity. The earth trembled like a monster mustering force.

A flare torpedoed from Yung Lu's tower. It scorched the sky and exploded into a cascade of sparks. Ryan spotted it first. He spun his head around and saw a twelve-foot-tall gorbot shoot out of a spout. It thundered down the mountain, a dozen smaller baboon-faced apes in its trail.

"Gorbots!" he yelled.

"I'll just zap 'em with some Shakespeare," groaned Lindsey, too zonked to get up.

"Aw, naw!" cried Ryan. "They've got their ears plugged!"

The ear-muffed apes charged toward them, and the trekkers riveted to a bolt upright, their hair on end.

"Slide!" shouted Ryan, hitching his haunches onto the gutter pipe. He pushed off using his rump as a bobsled. Lindsey and Oscar careened after him. The friction chafed their rear ends as if they were riding a scalding iron.

Ryan reached the base of the mountain first. Screaming his lungs out, he tore across the beachhead and dived into the iiiEnter-Prize. Chip revved up and veered to the rescue.

As Lindsey neared the base, the thunder engulfed her, and a

gorilla-shaped shadow intercepted her path. Panic-stricken, she whipped her head around.

"Don't look back!" shrieked Oscar, breathing hard on her neck. They sprang to their feet, hit the gravel, and raced toward the iiiEnter-Prize.

With only a few yards' dash between them and the macro-mouse, they streaked furiously across the beach. The gargantuan gorbot took a flying leap, hurtled itself over their heads, and spun around, cutting them off. Running so hard he couldn't rein his speed, Oscar skidded feet first into the hairy shins, stunning the beast.

"My glasses!" he shouted, wrestling to pick himself up.

With one hand Lindsey seized his wrist and wrenched him to his feet, with the other she scooped up a handful of gravel and shot it at the gorbot's eyes. Blinded and roaring, it took a swipe at her, and she was lucky to dodge its gigantic paw just as Chip floored the gas pedal and ripped into the back of its legs. The unexpected impact knocked the ape flat on its face. Lindsey shoved Oscar into the iiiEnter-Prize and jumped in after him. Chip gunned it full throttle. With the fuel-tank leaking and smoke curling from its snout, the injured macro-mouse took off at a hobble.

Lindsey looked back at the gorbots. "They're still coming!" she cried.

By now the shore was swarming with baboon-faced gorbots. They removed their ear-muffs to catch the plaintive squeals of the macro-mouse disappearing beneath the waves.

"They can tell we're in trouble!" screamed Ryan.

Like a team of synchronized swimmers, the creatures lined up, doubled over, belly-flopped into the surf, and dog-paddled in their wake.

"The steering's damaged," cried Chip. "I can't navigate."

The iiiEnter-Prize steamed up inside, swerved out of control, and smashed sidelong into the coral reef.

"Abandon ship!" commanded Ryan.

They unlatched the convertible top, floated to the surface, clamored onto the reef, and worked their way up. The apes roared after them. Lunging and plunging in sync, they flapped and kicked and bobbed over the rushing foam, splashing up jets of spray.

Richie whirled in overhead and tossed down the rope ladder. Chip nimbly hoisted himself aboard, and the trekkers tried to follow. With their last spurt of energy, they grabbed the ladder, looped their limbs through the ropes, and held on, swaying back and forth as the helicopter lifted off. Traumatized and unable to move, they dangled bug-eyed and helpless like three spiders freeze-drying on a web.

"Hey, Chipper," said Richie. "They're too wasted to climb."

The geeks dropped to the floor, peered out, and noticed that the rungs on the ladder weren't wide enough to hold two kids side by side.

"No way we can get down to them," said Richie. "We've got to pull them in one by one."

Their feet clamped into stirrups, their guts stretched to the breaking point, and with Alfred juiced to maximum voltage tugging and tooting, the geeks got the trekkers on board. With no time to spare, they reeled in the ladder before the gorbots could grab it. As the clipper-copter flew off, the angry gorbot growls receded into the surf, and the bedraggled trekkers sank into the hold, too shell-shocked to believe they'd escaped. Drained and dripping and tired beyond tears, they snuggled in their soggy basin. Not a whimper was heard as they soared to safety in silent stupor.

Chapter Sixteen

A TIME TO WEEP

Marie Celeste was in a royal blue funk, and Miss Prymm was grim. Newspapers were strewn all over the dining room table like bad report cards. Nobody mentioned the election results.

"Good morning," said Lindsey.

Judging from their red eyes and haggard faces, it was anything but a good morning. Not that Lindsey was in top form either. She'd gotten no sleep, and her knees and elbows were so badly bruised that she'd had to put on jeans and a long-sleeved shirt to hide the evidence – on the hottest day of the summer. She dragged herself to the table and dropped into her seat.

"YAWWW!" she cried, as her sore rear end struck the chair. She bounced back up again.

"That is no way to take your place at a table," said Marie Celeste. "And, while I'm at it, there's another matter I'd like to mention."

Lindsey blanched. Had her aunt heard the helicopter dropping her off?

"I happened to notice," continued the aunt, "that there's peanut brittle and toffee hidden in the kitchen cabinets."

It seemed that Lindsey was the only suspect, but Miss Prymm sank so deeply into her chair that her knees brushed against Lindsey's. She looked pathetic, and Lindsey couldn't help feeling sorry for her.

"Do you know anything about it?" said the aunt, her eyes fixed on Lindsey.

"Yes, Aunt Marie Celeste."

"So, you've been *chewing* behind my back. That's very

naughty of you. You'll have no more pudding until you start be-having like a lady again."

Miss Prymm gave Lindsey a hangdog look of undying grati-tude, and Lindsey flashed her a grin.

"How did the election go?" she asked, picking up The Elsi-nore X-Press.

"Weary, flat, stale, and unprofitable," muttered the aunt. "Chronicles of wasted time."

"Wasted time," whispered Miss Prymm.

Marie Celeste was in no mood for idle chatter. She fluttered her fingertips at the top headline. It read: STARTLING CHECK-MATE VICTORY!

"Dr. Mandher lost?"

"He won and lost," said the aunt in a vexed tone. "If you'd watch more television, you wouldn't need to pester me with so many questions."

"So who's the winner?" said Lindsey, more intrigued by puz-zles than by politics.

"Mayor Mandher."

"I don't get it."

"I find it distasteful to talk about ill-gotten gains, Lindsey, but I suppose that I should be pleased that you are finally benefiting from a sound education and displaying an interest in something important."

"Important," said Miss Prymm.

"It was those teeth of his. Somebody got hold of the smiling photo flyers and plastered them all over a special edition of The Elsinore X-Press, which was distributed outside the poll booths. By the time I discovered the ploy, it was too late."

"So Mrs. Blooper won?"

"Heavens no, Lindsey. Her majority-making constituents spent the night in jail. The Blue Brigade caught their animals loitering on private property, and the owners were charged with trespassing. Criminals aren't permitted to vote, you know. We worked for hours shredding their ballots – by hand, of all things. Fleecer's ballot-bulldozing machine got jammed. Evidentially, it wasn't built to meet the needs of a technologically advanced democracy."

"So Dr. Mandher won?"

Marie Celeste nodded. "Only to be ousted within minutes. Forced to resign. A certain not-to-be-mentioned relative of mine, who happens to be the leader of the Pink Party, called for a referendum vote to remove so-called "crooked" candidates from office. Unfortunately, almost everybody had seen Dr. Mandher's teeth. They look as if he'd been force-fed bicycle spokes, and the serious photo flyers I distributed didn't fool a soul."

"Fool a soul," said Miss Prymm.

"Who is the new mayor?" asked Lindsey.

"Mrs. Mandher."

"She was running against her husband?"

"Of course not. She was one of the few Paradisians who didn't run against him. Seven hundred sixty-two people declared themselves candidates – a shameful display. Then Chief Justice Imelda ruled that the mayor's term of office had to be completed by the next of kin. It's in the family values bylaws."

"The next of kin?" asked Lindsey.

"The closest relative, Mrs. Mandher."

"And her teeth are straight?" Lindsey started thinking Ryan might become the next mayor.

"Perfectly," said the aunt. "You're not to go gallivanting all over town this morning. I've scheduled an appointment with the tailor at twelve noon. Punctually. It's about time we got you outfitted like a lady."

Lindsey added a dollop of honey to her cereal and polished it off.

"If you've finished your breakfast, you'd better step out onto the verandah. There's a girl waiting for you. Do not invite her into the house until her feet dry. And kindly don't disturb me for the rest of the morning. Miss Prymm and I have a great deal to do. There are only six days left until the next election."

*

When Lindsey stepped outdoors, she found Cerise with her feet propped on the banister, painting her toenails. She tossed Lindsey a bashful smile.

"Cerise, what are you doing here?"

"I wanted to see you. You don't mind, do you? I'm not speaking to the Bond brothers, and I got awful lonesome." Cerise produced a package of bubble gum and held it out like a peace offering. "Want a stick of Dumbot's Delight?"

Without so much as a passing thought toward etiquette lesson number one, Lindsey took the gum, popped it into her mouth, and chewed away.

"Where's Ryan?" she said.

"At K⁴CC."

It appeared that he hadn't told Cerise about Mission Mount Cinderella, probably afraid she'd tell the oldies. Funny how the kids would rather face gorbots than oldies, but keeping stuff from adults had become a way of life – and it was beginning to bother her the way everything seemed to be built on secrets with the kids risking their lives while everybody kept pretending that nothing was wrong on Paradise.

It would be lots easier to pin down the oldies and make them give us some answers, thought Lindsey. Sure, they're weird and difficult, but they aren't exactly the enemy. Lindsey wished she could call Ryan to talk things over. She had plenty to discuss with him, but she'd have to wait until Cerise left, and Cerise wasn't budging. She was unnaturally still, staring into space like a zombie.

With every muscle complaining, Lindsey eased herself into a seat and gazed out at Azure Avenue. A marathon of oldies was jogging by with Juanita Shringapur and Rosie neck and neck at the lead. Lindsey noticed Poochie and Johnny Blooper, Squeaky Zeitung, Captain Friedman, and others. Trailing them was a makeshift ambulance with Fleecer at the wheel, his rates clearly posted on the door.

I bet Fleecer can sell us some stun-guns, thought Lindsey, storing the idea away for future reference.

She heard Cerise sniffling and turned toward her. "Boy troubles?" she asked.

"No," said Cerise. Her lower lip trembled into a sad little smile. "I think Rhett likes me."

"What's the problem?"

"Can you please help me? I don't know who to turn to, and you're so brave."

"Me? Brave?"

"The way you saved us from those horrible gorbots. I don't dare go to the beach any more without you, and I just want to say how awful bad I feel 'cuz I voted against you."

"No problem," said Lindsey, feeling magnanimous. It struck her that Cerise might be pretty mentally challenged, but she was basically a good kid. "What can I do for you?"

"Help me get my canary back?"

"Your canary?"

"Yes. It's a little yellow bird with a yellow body, and a yellow head and tail, and yellow wings."

"Uh-huh."

"And feathers."

"Yellow?" asked Lindsey, trying to keep a straight face.

"Yes."

"Where is it?"

"Jack's got it. He's been blackmailing me," said Cerise in a tragic tone. "He found out about my poem. But it doesn't matter now that everybody knows."

"What poem?"

"'Thirty Days Has September.' He went over to the airport and read the visitors' register and found out I got into Paradise by reciting the first two verses. It's the only poetry I know," said Cerise miserably.

"They let you in with two lines of *that*?" Lindsey was appalled.

"My Great Granny Ellis is the immigration officer," said Cerise.

"Oh."

"You'll help me? I miss my poor little Birdie so much."

"Sure," said Lindsey. "Friends got to stick together."

"I'm so glad we're friends. You'll write me when we get home?"

"I'll need your address. I don't even know your last name...."

"It's Einstein."

Cerise rummaged through her tote bag, took out her address book and pen, and handed them to Lindsey.

Lindsey started writing, and Cerise began hunting for her toe-nail gloss, unaware that a mega-gorbot was lurking behind a rhododendron bush. Before Lindsey could scream, let alone recite any Shakespeare, the creature tiptoed out of the bushes and gagged her. It swept her into its arms, leaped over the fence, and disappeared as Cerise watched in horror.

"Lindsey! Help! Help! Lindsey! Thirty days has September!" she shouted, and she dissolved into a flood of tears.

"What is this commotion?" cried the aunt, bursting out the door in a most unladylike fashion.

"Lindseeeey! WHAAAAAAAH! Septeeeember!" sobbed Cerise, and she wept so loudly and so long that it took Marie Celeste a full fifteen minutes to discover what had happened.

*

Lindsey would never recall exactly what took place next. All that lingered in her mind was a blur of sensations: the crush of synthetic fur against her skin, an acrid prickle in her nostrils, the tread of heavy feet, and the rock-hard paws cradling her so tightly that she could barely move. She was terrified. Her mouth went dry under the gag. With a sharp intake of breath, her bubble gum shot down her throat and got painfully lodged. Unable to spit it out, she swallowed it.

Squashed against the gorbot's chest, she could see nothing, but she could tell she was traveling at a fast clip over land and then water, inside the stifling belly of a moby-modem hydro-jet cutting across the sea and slowing as it reached shore. She could hear the waves slapping against the hull. Once again, she felt the bumping gait of the gorbot and realized she was on dry land. She heard the crunch of gravel underfoot and the clatter of pebbles as her captor scaled the steep slopes of the volcano.

Raucous screeches filled the air. The gorbot paused to reshuffle Lindsey under one arm. The change of position gave her enough leeway to crane her neck and see the sky blacken with grackle birds rolling in like storm clouds. She watched them in grim fascination.

The cawing grew shrill. The crazed birds swirled and gyrated, working themselves into an assault formation. The gorbot continued plodding uphill, flailing its free arm to ward them off. Keeping its eyes skyward, the gorbot came to a halt and began kicking the crusty surface until a trap door swung open like a spout exposing a chute that thrust deep into the earth. Before the creature could duck inside, the frenzied birds attacked, savagely biting and clawing. The gorbot reared in rage and thrashed at their tough, sinewy bodies.

Pinned and wriggling under a burly arm, Lindsey was shielded from their beaks but half smothered, struggling for air. As she wrestled to get away, the gag loosened, and she let off a scream. Thick fingers muzzled her mouth, and she sank her teeth in. She felt the grip slacken, and suddenly she was free.

The grackle birds retreated to launch another attack. Lindsey hitched onto the gutter pipe and pushed off only to feel herself snatched back by a giant paw. In a flash, she was shoved through the trap door and tumbling down a chute into the bowels of the Inferno.

*

Lindsey hit bottom and found herself sprawled on the floor of a cave. Overhead the battle between the gorbot and the grackles was still raging. Their cries ricocheted off the walls, hollow as a nightmare returning to haunt her. Her ears were ringing, and she ached all over, but none of her bones seemed to be broken. As her eyes adjusted, her first thought was to escape.

From where she was, swathed in a phosphorescent light, she could see that the cave opened into passageways. In a fit of panic, she tore down one of them, heedless of where she was going. Madly she ran, propelled by fear, picking up speed, scraping her flesh against the bruising darkness, and bouncing back into the fall line. The going was slippery, and she was so out of control that she barely noticed the tunnel narrowing like a sleeve about to bend. Too late, she realized she was heading into a stone wall. She lost her footing and crashed.

The impact brought tears to her eyes. To steady herself, she rested her palms against the wall. It was overgrown with moss, clammy and loathsome to the touch. Waves of nausea forced her to her knees. She felt moisture on her cheeks, realized she was crying, and abandoned herself to tears, weeping as if life itself hung on the fury of the downpour.

When the storm inside her subsided, she lay curled on the floor unable to move, listening to her own breathing, and pretending to be safe at home.

The silence that engulfed her was nerve-wracking. She was at the point of screaming when a voice inside her cried, "THINK!"

Think? Her head was spinning. A confusion of words buffeted her. Alarming words. Dark, wheel-like, turning clouds of words spun out of nowhere and gathered into a warning: *Fear is the deadliest demon!*

What did it mean? She felt helpless. THINK!

Through sheer willpower, she pulled her mind into focus and realized that fear itself was pushing her deeper into danger. Panic was suicidal. She risked getting hurt, lost, and trapped in a labyrinth of interlocking tunnels. She had no hope of being rescued – nobody knew where she was. She'd have to rely on her wits to find a way out, and the sole way out might be the way she'd come in.

She needed a hiding place and looked around to assess her situation. Behind her lay the tunnel she'd come down – her only sure way back. On either side of her branching out at sharp angles were smaller, gloomier tunnels. She'd have to take one, but which?

If I always follow the fork to the right, she told herself, I can retrace my steps by sticking to the left and then climb back up the shoot and escape once it's safe. Forming a plan bolstered her courage, and she began to move ahead with a sense of purpose, scouring the slimy walls for a place to conceal herself – a boulder or a crevice, anything big enough to crouch behind or squeeze into.

The gag was still dangling from her throat, and she used it to wipe the slime from her hands. The gag! With a shiver of excitement, she realized she was no longer muzzled, and she could neutralize the gorbot with a poem. If only she'd thought of that sooner, she could have stopped herself from being pushed down the chute. And there was no longer any need to run, no need to risk getting lost. All she had to do was stand firm and recite a few lines. She knew she could do it.

Without so much as a tremor, she turned around and headed back only to hear the booming echo of footsteps and a blood-curdling roar. Was it a gorbot or something else? There was no way to tell. A ripple of fear shot through her; she panicked and bolted. Through the coal-dark underground she fled, her eyes fixed on a far off blade of light until she found herself at a dead end, facing a door. Heart in throat, she turned the handle and was met by a blast of air. The stench of dying roses overpowered her. She covered her face and passed out.

Chapter Seventeen

LOVE'S LABOUR'S LOST

The he fog came on little cat feet. It cut off the visibility on every island of the archipelago. Meanwhile Lindsey lay semi-conscious on a cool bed, dozing off into dreams of tiglons and ostriches and buffaloes chomping through lychee-fruit groves. When she came to her senses, she had no idea where she was.

Eyes gluey and head aching, she stretched out a hand, parted a set of drapes, and looked around. Her first impression was that she was on the inside of a monstrous goldfish bowl. Mist clung like cotton candy against the transparent wall.

Within the dim enclosure, she could distinguish shadowy, motionless figures. She dragged herself to her feet, groped along the wall until she felt a light switch, turned it on, and found herself in a majestic bed chamber, the walls studded with bright stones like the inside of a jewelry box. From the ceiling, a chandelier shaped like the planet Saturn loomed above her, dwarfing her, and flooding the room with light. She blinked, but the vision seemed real.

Never had she beheld such opulence. Everything was oversized and overbearing. She ran her eyes around the room and saw a poster bed, larger-than-life statues, and a massive desk and chair. She touched the surfaces to test if she was dreaming, and she came across a heart-shaped box of chocolates. The card by it read, "To the most beautiful girl ever born, from her loving Jedgar."

Lindsey nearly swooned dead away.

A gruff voice came over the intercom. "Are you awake, my darling?"

"Who's there?" she gasped.

"I'll have Ariel bring you to the dining room."

Lindsey staggered into the bathroom and found a fountain spouting arches of water. She splashed her face and drank deeply. Greatly refreshed, she turned around and discovered a robot, no larger than a hummingbird, hovering overhead.

"I'm Ariel," twittered the tiny apparition, flapping its napkin-white wings. "Follow me."

Ariel led her down the subterranean palace through caverns measureless to man. Along the lonely corridors, she caught glimpses of richly appointed halls that appeared to gawk at her in hollow-eyed splendor. Nobody seemed to live there, nothing looked alive, and the air was so stuffy that even the artificial flowers hung from their stalks as if wilting. She took a deep breath and felt the mustiness rush into her lungs, dulling her senses.

Lindsey fell into such deep meditation that she barely noticed her surroundings. She was certain she was on the inside of Mount Cinderella, and the source of the mysteries lay buried in this treasure-filled tomb. Her eyelids drooped, and her legs mechanically propelled her like a conveyor belt drawing her through a slow-moving particle of time. Blindly, she followed the lifeless path down to the Jedgar's lair.

From the depths, a rough beast slouched toward her, a shape with lion body and the head of man, a gaze blank and pitiless as the sun. It rose before her, mesmerizing her and rendering her powerless. Unable to stop herself, she kept moving closer and closer to the beast.

With a jolt, she realized she was caught in a tide of imagination. She shook herself out of the trance. As her eyes refocused, the dreadful image vanished, and once again she saw her feathery guide fluttering ahead through lavish hallways. She whispered a silent prayer and told herself to be brave. Instinctively, she pressed her hand to her heart and felt it beating boldly.

At long last, they came to a halt before an archway hung with tapestries.

"I'm so glad you're here," chirped Ariel. "My poor master has been so unhappy waiting for you. I was afraid he'd die of sorrow."

The tiny herald pulled out a miniature trumpet to announce their arrival, and the tapestries drew apart. Steady, steady, with a strange heart-beating calm, Lindsey stepped through the entrance into a candle-lit dining hall with a thirty-foot-long table that seemed to slope away from her. No chairs lined it. Instead, a throne piled high with cushions had been placed at each end. And on the nether throne sat the Jedgar.

At the sight of Lindsey, he jumped from his seat and hurried toward her with his arms outstretched in welcome. It was a long walk from one end of the table to the other, and Lindsey had plenty of time to look him over.

He was a chubby, clean-shaven, old man with ruddy cheeks and a shiny nose. Even though his hair was white, the color of his complexion made him look like a well-scrubbed infant mistakenly wearing a necktie in place of a bib. His eyes twinkled, and he smiled expectantly. Just before he reached her, he stopped short.

"You're not my Rosie!" he cried in a devastated tone. He dropped to the floor with a thump and started banging his head against the polished marble.

Lindsey's eyes widened. She had never seen a grown man in such a state. Under different circumstances, she might have felt pity, but *he* wasn't the victim, *she* was. He didn't seem to notice her or care about the terrible ordeal he'd put her through. As her astonishment turned to outrage, she grew red in the face. She felt like kicking him and screaming, "What about ME?"

The more she thought about it, the more her blood boiled. She was ripping mad, angrier than she'd ever been in her life. Elsinore was in turmoil, and the oldies were all stressed out, and the kids had been grounded half the summer — all because of this selfish, slobbering lump on the floor. And he wasn't even sorry, except for himself.

He's nothing but a cry baby, she thought furiously, a miserable old man who makes everybody else miserable too. Somebody should have put a stop to him.

"Stop it!" she cried.

He got to his feet and pulled himself to his full height, which wasn't a whole lot taller than Lindsey.

"You're not my Rosie," he repeated, shifting the blame onto her as if she'd purposely tricked him. "I'm sending you back."

"No, you're not!" The look on her face was fierce. She'd been pushed around far too long, and she wasn't about to put up with it. "You're not getting away with this!"

"Gorbots!" he called, and gorbots of all sizes herded through the archway. "Take her back!"

A furry arm scooped her into the air.

"No!" she screamed. She mustered her strength and punched the gorbot in the nose. The creature dropped her, and she landed squarely on her feet. "I'll destroy every gorbot you've got!" she cried, frantically trying to recall some poetry.

The gorbots backed off, and the Jedgar looked vulnerable as if suddenly stripped of his armor.

Lindsey was so furious that she was trembling, but her eyes were steady. "You're *nothing* without your gorillas and your volcano! You're going to answer to me, or I'll *do* something to you!"

She had no idea what she could *do* to him, but she was too angry to think. She stared at him with her fists clenched, and he stared back in shock as the vaguely defined threat sank in. It was a standoff. Her eyes blazed into his until he flinched and looked away.

"You look so much like Rosie," he whispered.

"So what!" She was still raging. "You kidnapped me! And you meant to kidnap my aunt! You're a horrid old bully!"

"You're Rosie's niece?"

"I'm Lindsey O'Neill, and I've had it with you!"

She'd never spoken to an adult that way, but he was wrong, and she was right, and there was no stopping her.

"I had a good reason," he said, unrepentant.

"Big deal!" It infuriated her to think of the things he'd done.

"I've never kidnapped anybody before."

"Stop making trouble or else!" she hissed.

There was a long, tense pause as they glared at each other. She noticed the expression on his face gradually changing. He was regaining his self-confidence and didn't intend to back down. He dusted himself off, fluffed up his voluminous necktie, and watched her with a cagey look on his face.

"Or else what?" he asked.

"Or else..." The challenge took her off guard. "Or else..." She had a sudden inspiration, and she took a wild stab. "Or else I'll make you sorry about the gold earrings!"

"Oh, no!" he yelped. She'd struck a sore spot. He shrank so small that he seemed to be imploding. "The earrings! My only link to Rosie!"

Lindsey dug in her heels. He could carry on as much as he liked, but she wasn't giving in.

"Rosie," he sobbed, as if his heart were breaking. "I want my Rosie!"

He cried and cried and cried. As water puts out fire, his tears slowly wore her down, draining her resolve. Although it looked like nothing but self-pity, the outpouring was effective. She felt herself weakening.

Then she remembered the golden mean like a gift her mother had left her, and she saw right through him.

He's manipulating me, playing on my feelings, she realized, and he thinks he can get away with it because I'm a kid. As she rallied her willpower, it dawned on her that she had more inner resources than he did. She had to gain the upper hand – the fate of Paradise was riding on her.

"Stop the trouble right now." Her tone was steely. "Right this minute, and then maybe, just maybe, I'll think about helping you."

A ray of hope flickered in his watery blue eyes. "What can you do to help me?"

"Swear to undo the mess you've made."

"Can you help me get Rosie back?"

"No more trouble? Word of honor!" She wasn't giving an inch, and he nodded in abject surrender.

"Word of honor," he said.

"You owe me a big apology. I want to hear you say you're sorry."

He shuffled his feet and scowled and mumbled under his breath. Lindsey nailed him with a look.

"I'm sorry," he said in a tiny voice.

"I didn't hear that very well," said she.

"I'M SORRY!"

"You owe an apology to every single person in Paradise. And the damage you've caused – you'd better clean it up. Clear?"

He nodded grimly. "What about Rosie?"

"Tell me your story, and we'll see."

He picked up her throne, carried it the full length of the table, and placed it next to his.

"Sit beside me, little one, and I'll tell you my sad, sad tale."

With a soulful air, he turned toward the candelabra and lost himself in its tear-shaped flames.

*

"When I was a mere lad of twelve," began the Jedgar, his eyes glowing in the mellow light, "I made a discovery – love. I fell in love, wholly and irrevocably, for the one and only time. A sweet-smelling girl with Titian-red hair stole my heart away. Her name was Rosie O'Neill, and she swore that she loved me too. I was the happiest boy on earth.

"But then," he said ominously, "we went into seventh grade, and we joined the Drama Club. We tried out for parts in *The Tempest*, a Shakespearean play she adores. She was Miranda, and I was Caliban. We rehearsed every day together, and for a while my life was bliss.

"At Christmas I gave her a pair of gold earrings shaped like rosebuds. She told me she didn't like jewelry – all she wanted was fun. But she promised she'd wear them till the day we wed, and she gave me a kiss on the nose." He pointed to a spot on the tip of his cherry-red nose.

"She still wears the earrings," murmured Lindsey.

The Jedgar exhaled an anguished sigh. "She always keeps her word, she does, my wonderful, wonderful Rose."

The gorbots positioned themselves along the wall like a chorus line awaiting instructions. Lindsey hoped the Jedgar would order something to eat. She was hungry and thirsty, but mostly she wanted to hear his story.

"Out!" thundered the Jedgar, shooing the gorbots away, and they lumbered off with their tails tucked between their legs.

Lindsey pulled her throne closer to the Jedgar and waited for him to continue.

"Where was I?" he asked.

"She gave you a kiss on the nose."

He touched the tip of his nose with his index finger and kept it there for several moments as if trying to locate his train of thought.

"Ah," he said. "Then the hard times came. After the Christmas vacation, I was thrown out of Drama Club. I couldn't learn my lines. I tried and tried every day, but I couldn't remember the words. It was then that Rosie broke up with me. She told me she'd never be true to one who lacked poetry in his heart. And she promised she'd take me back the day I learned a Shakespearean sonnet. I've been trying ever since."

"For sixty years?" Lindsey was agog. "You've been at it for sixty years!"

"Anything for my Rosie."

"But a sonnet is only fourteen lines long. If you'd learned one line every four years you'd already know it by now."

"I'm a failure!"

"The course of true love never did run smooth," she said gravely.

The Jedgar grew moist with tears, and she pretended not to notice as he sopped them up with his necktie.

"There's something else I've never confessed." He wretchedly twisted the necktie and squeezed the excess water into his finger bowl. "I did something really bad."

"Share it with me, poor Jedgar," she said, deeply moved.

"I was so desperate that I committed the unpardonable. I had to know if Rosie still cared for me, so I took to snooping on her. She caught me reading her diary, and she turned into a fury. She said she wouldn't marry me if I was the last person on earth. And she stamped her foot."

"That was very wrong of you," said Lindsey. "You should be ashamed of yourself."

"I know, I know. I hate myself, but I just couldn't help it. I'm an incurable nosy-body. It's in my blood. And all I could think of was Rosie, my beautiful, beautiful Rose."

The Jedgar jumped from his throne and paced back and forth in such distress that he was unable to continue.

"Please tell me the rest," she said, and he sagged back into his throne.

"Where was I?" he asked, slipping into another senior moment.

"Beautiful Rose."

He pressed his button nose again and nodded. "Well, we both grew up. She kept getting married to everybody who proposed, but *not* to me. She had six husbands. The last one was an Arab named Sheik Espir. When he introduced himself to her, she thought he said 'Shakespeare' so she married him. I was beside myself." The Jedgar pounded himself on the temple.

"You seem to know everything about her."

"It's my business to know. I'm a secret agent at heart, not a poet. Got the best espionage organization in the world to help me track my Rosie."

"You're a professional spy?"

"Top of the breed. As a young man, I went to Washington, D.C. and joined the intelligence service. By the time I retired, I was running the place. Perhaps you've heard of me. My real name is J. Edgar –"

"J. Edgar? Not Jedgar?"

"The keypunch operators at work kept getting it wrong and running the whole thing together. All the printouts read 'Jedgar' instead of 'J. Edgar,' so before long everybody started calling me the Jedgar, and it stuck. But my real name is J. Edgar Lectrolux."

"No!" Lindsey was floored.

"Yes! And I've spent my life chasing Rosie, the only girl of my dreams."

Lindsey sank back into the goose-down cushions, and the Jedgar jumped to his feet.

"Rosie!" he cried, running in circles around the table. "Come back to me, Rosie!"

His voice rang through the regal dining hall and along the luxurious corridors of the palace, and despite the ostentation, and despite the wealth and glitter, the whole place seemed empty.

*

Pensioners' Paradise was in an uproar. Never in history, to the last syllable of recorded time, had a child ever been lost. The Pinks, the Whites, and the Blues forgot all about important issues and collaborated in the search. Oldies and kids flocked into Elsinore from the outlying islands, and the population in the capital tripled.

Ryan discovered that there were over a dozen kids on the far sides of Paradise, and they all joined the Rangers. Everyone pitched in on the hunt, that is everyone but Cerise who spent the day silk-screening T-shirts for the new recruits.

On Jedgar's Inferno itself, J. Edgar Lectrolux pushed his solid gold fork around his dinner plate in utter dejection.

"I've got a sneaking suspicion that this is my very last chance," he said, dropping his face into his hands.

"What?" shouted Lindsey. She could barely hear him from her end of the thirty-foot-long table.

He picked up a megaphone and directed his voice at her. "I've got a sneaking suspicion that this is my very last chance!"

A gorbot, clad only in white gloves, a crisply folded napkin over one wrist, and a pair of patent leather shoes with gold buckles, nipped around the table filling the centerpieces with tropical fruit. Using silver tongs, the gorbot selected a ripe banana and daintily peeled it for Lindsey. She was quite impressed by such elegant living.

"Can I call my aunt?" she asked. By now Marie Celeste was bound to be in a snit.

"No diplomatic channels between Inferno and Paradise," he said sulkily. "I'll send a gorbot when the fog lifts."

"Didn't *you* cause the fog?"

"Not this time. Pure act of nature."

"You've caused plenty of trouble in Paradise. How could you *do* such terrible things?"

"I'll have to show you the control room."

"That's not what I meant," she said with a stern look, but it crossed her mind that she should make a point of visiting the control room before she left. She had lots of questions to ask.

"Nobody's ever gotten hurt," he said, "unless you count the time that Miss Prymm cracked a wisdom tooth."

Lindsey pictured Miss Prymm trying to explain how she managed to crack a tooth on a mouthful of pudding.

"You've been a real nuisance," said Lindsey.

"They called me a non-person and pretended I didn't exist. They thought I'd go away. But I won't, and I won't, and I won't!"

She'd heard that line before. From Rosie. It sounded as if all of Paradise had gotten caught up in the tug of war between two oldies — a stubborn old woman and a stubborn old man.

"So you started causing trouble. No wonder nobody likes you," she yelled. The distance between them was beginning to strain her vocal chords.

"I know, I know. But I'm not a deadbeat. I'm an honorable man, and I always pay for my sins. Righting Yung Lu's tower will cost me a pretty penny."

"And the flood damage?"

"It's my terrible temper. I've been paying for it all my life. When I think about not seeing Rosie, I sometimes get so angry I can't control myself."

"What about Shakespeare? You gave the statue a black eye?"

"I cannot tell an untruth," he said, lowering his voice to a tone of wounded righteousness. "I did not do that."

"But one of your gorbots did." Lindsey sighed in dismay. "It's amazing that Rosie cares about you at all."

"She still loves me?"

"I'm sure she does, but she hates your awful Inferno. She thinks you built it out of spite."

"Out of spite? I built it to impress her, to make her take me seriously. I wanted to show her how rich and powerful I've become. It took me a year of hard work plus millions and millions of dollars to build this citadel, this stately pleasure dome, this castle."

And it made you feel big and important, she thought, but it did no good at all. How could an intelligent person go so far wrong? He didn't understand the first thing about Rosie.

"You heard what she said about the earrings? She doesn't give a hoot about jewelry and stuff, and macho power-plays turn her right off. You've got to give her what *she* wants."

"I'll buy her anything."

Lindsey shook her head sadly. He still didn't get the picture. "You said she'd take you back if you memorized a sonnet."

"A poem!" He slammed his fist on the table. He was a very stubborn old man, but the O'Neills were just as stubborn. Maybe more.

"You'll learn one," said Lindsey, convinced that he could do it. Mr. J. Edgar Lectrolux, one of the smartest men in the world, had to be able learn a sonnet.

He's bright and motivated, she observed, recalling the teacher jargon she'd heard at school. It's a question of readiness for learning. With a little friendly help and a touch of ingenuity, the poem should stick like glue....

Ariel fluttered in. "Dear Master, I'll put on some Christmas music to cheer you."

The Jedgar nodded absently. "Christmas music always reminds me of that heavenly day when Rosie kissed my nose."

"Jingle bells, jingle bells, jingle all the way," piped the stereo box, and the unhappy man droned along.

Lindsey listened with a perplexed expression on her face. She had the fleeting sensation that the answer was right there in front of her if only she could decipher it, and she tried to concentrate while he kept on singing.

"Oh what fun it is to ride in a one horse open sleigh..."

As she stared at the Jedgar, she remembered that Rosie had said something about "the nose knows." It's right in front of his nose, she thought, and words can stick like glue....

"That's it!" she cried, sprinting the full length of the table to join him. "You know the WORDS!"

"Ummm," went the Jedgar.

"You can memorize!"

"What do you mean?"

"I mean, if you can learn a song, you can learn a sonnet."

"You think I can learn a sonnet?"

"If you sing it, you can," she laughed. "Montezuma's Miracle is yummy, yummy, yummy!"

He gave her an odd look.

"Don't you see?" she said. "Lyrics are like poetry, and music can make a poem stick like glue."

The Jedgar perked up. "And I can go to Pensioners' Paradise and see Rosie?"

"What's to stop you?"

"The immigration lady...."

"You have a copy of *The Complete Works of William Shakespeare*?" she asked.

"I've always cherished it. Rosie gave it to me that first Christmas when I gave her the rosebud earrings. I keep it in there." He pointed at a fancily carved hope chest covered with a thick layer of dust. It looked as if it hadn't been opened for a very long time, but Lindsey was wise enough not to comment.

"Let's get to work," she said, her dimples gleaming. And for the first time in sixty years, the Jedgar looked truly hopeful.

*

"Done," said Lindsey, flashing the scroll she'd been working on. "I've scanned a sonnet so that it fits the beats to 'Jingle Bells.' It's easy to sing if you follow the markings. I capitalized the stresses and underlined the words that have to be stretched out."

With a satisfied grin, she handed him the scroll. The Jedgar compared the parallel verses with the version in his Shakespeare book.

"You've stuck in four O's that aren't in the poem," he objected.

"I had to – it was the only way I could make it fit right. But it should be okay. I mean, an 'O' is a zero," she said, flaunting her logical mind, "and everybody knows that when you add in a zero it doesn't change anything."

"Logic isn't Rosie's strong point," he said, unconvinced.

"Trust me. We will do it come what will come!" cried Lindsey, and together they sang:

O—shall I	JINgle BELLS
COMpare THEE	JINgle BELLS

TO a SUMmer's DAY	JINgle ALL the WAY
THOU art MORE	OH what FUN
LOveLY	It IS to RIDE
AND more TEMperATE	In a ONE horse OPen SLEIGH
O—rough WINDS	JINgle BELLS
DO shake THE	JINgle BELLS
DARling BUDS of MAY	JINgle ALL the WAY
And SUMmer's LEASE	OH what FUN
HATH	It IS to RIDE
ALL too SHORT a DATE	In a ONE horse OPen SLEIGH
O—someTIME too HOT	DASHing THROUGH the SNOW
The EYE of HEAven SHINES	On a ONE horse OPen SLEIGH
And OFten IS HIS	O'ER the FIELDS we GO
GOLD comPLExion dimMED	LAUGHing ALL the WAY
And EVery FAIR from FAIR	BELLS on BOBtails RING
SOMETIME deCLINES	MAKing SPIRits BRIGHT
By CHANCE or	What FUN it IS
NAture's	To LAUGH and SING
CHANGing COURSE unTRIMMED	A SLEIGHing SONG toNIGHT
O—but THY	JINgle BELLS
EterNAL	JINgle BELLS
SUMmer SHALL not FADE	JINgle ALL the WAY
NOR LOSE	OH what FUN
POSsesSION	It IS to RIDE
OF That FAIR thou OW'ST	In a ONE horse OPen SLEIGH
NOR shall DEATH	JINgle BELLS
BRAG THOU	JINgle BELLS
WANder'st IN his SHADE	JINgle ALL the WAY
WHEN in ETERNAL	OH what FUN it IS to RIDE
LINES to TIME thou GROW'ST	In a ONE horse OPen SLEIGH
So LONG as MEN can BREATHE	DASHing THROUGH the SNOW
OR EYES can SEE	On a ONE horse OPen SLEIGH
So LONG LIVES THIS	O'ER the FIELDS we GO
And THIS gives LIFE to THEE	LAUGHing ALL the WAY

(refrain)

So LONG as MEN can BREATHE	BELLS on BOBtail RING
OR EYES can SEE	MAKing SPIrits Bright
So LONG	What FUN it IS
LIVES THIS	To LAUGH and SING
And THIS gives LIFE to THEE!	A SLEIGHing SONG toNIGHT!

It was rough going at first, and they both stumbled, but before long the Jedgar got the hang of it, and they finished the duet splendidly. After several rehearsals, he was even beginning to like it, and he managed to perform it without a hitch.

She stuck out her hand to take the scroll. "Now try doing it from memory," she said.

"Can't I just read it?" he asked. His knuckles whitened as he clutched the scroll to his breast.

"You want to cheat!"

"It isn't exactly cheating. It's like a teleprompter. She'll never know the difference."

"Yes, she will." Rosie might be a ding-dong, but she wasn't stupid. If he cheated, she'd figure it out fast. "Put the scroll away and recite your sonnet!"

The Jedgar nodded. He seemed to be warming up, and he pressed his finger to his nose.

"Ready?" she asked.

"Let me try it this way," he said, tapping his nose.

He was asking *her* permission!

"You want to recite Shakespeare with your finger on your nose?" she giggled.

"Why not? It helps me to concentrate."

Why not, indeed? Lindsey had to admit that his approach made sense in a ditzy sort of way. After all, he was a professional nose. Who could blame him for using his greatest asset?

"Well, if it works for you," she said grandly, "go for it."

For the rest of the evening, she coached him and spurred him on until she felt her eyes glazing over, and she heard herself saying, "Attaboy," which sounded pretty disrespectful, but he didn't seem to mind. At the stroke of midnight, he threw on a master switch that lit up Mount Cinderella like a pumpkin, and he announced that he knew the whole sonnet by heart. And Lindsey was worn to a frazzle.

"Good night, sweet Lindsey O'Neill," said he. "Ariel will show you the way to soft, dreamless sleep."

"Good night, dear Uncle Jedgar," said she. And she gave him a kiss on the tip of his cherry-red nose.

Chapter Eighteen

LOVE'S LABOUR'S WON

When rosy-fingered dawn caressed the horizon, the shores of Elsinore harbor looked like a traffic jam. Every sea-worthy vessel and every air carrier in Paradise was lined along the ports and poised to invade the Inferno. Ryan's Rangers were decked out in their pink, white, and blue T-shirts, and the geeks from K⁴CC were instructing them how to operate a fleet of macromice with souped-up search engines geared to splice through the invisible barrier.

Dizzy with anticipation, dumbots and robots spruced themselves up to pose for the PPU cameras. Oldies hummed and hawed, eagerly testing the engines of their floating and flying machines. Yung Lu, too impatient to remain idle, polished his sampan with his pigtail as he awaited the blast of Sally Mandher's starter pistol. And the entire Blue Brigade readied itself for combat by issuing honorary badges to all participants.

Suddenly the nozzle of Mount Cinderella swiveled to point straight at Elsinore. The giant crater – refitted during the night with a wall-to-wall amplifier – boomed from its subterranean sound studio. The tune was "Jingle Bells," the words were Shakespeare's, and the voice was unmistakably the Jedgar's.

> O—Shall I compare thee to a summer's day?
> Thou art more lovely and more temperate.
> O—Rough winds do shake the darling buds of May,
> And summer's lease hath all too short a date.
> O—Sometime too hot the eye of heaven shines,
> And often is his gold complexion dimmed,
> And every fair from fair sometime declines,

By chance or nature's changing course untrimmed;
O—But thy eternal summer shall not fade
Nor lose possession of that fair thou ow'st,
Nor shall death brag thou wander'st in his shade
When in eternal lines to time thou grow'st.
  So long as men can breathe or eyes can see,
  So long lives this, and this gives life to thee!

Cataclysmic moments give rise to unpredictable reactions. Along the boardwalks, the Rangers were dumbstruck, but Cerise, who had trained as a cheerleader, instantly latched onto the beat.

"Come on, y'all!" she shouted, kicking up her heels to form a conga line.

She grabbed Rhett, who grabbed Ryan, who grabbed Chip, who grabbed Richie, who grabbed Jack, who grabbed Oscar, who grabbed Zach, who grabbed the first pretty girl he saw, who grabbed the next new Ranger until every kid in Paradise was hopping and kicking to the rhythm.

An equal but opposite reaction took place amongst the oldies. There was barely a dry eye as they listened to the recital. Never before had an abuser of the world, a practicer of arts inhibited, made such a dramatic conversion. Bardolatry waxed triumphant!

"O O O O that Shakespeherian Rag!" sang Yung Lu.

"It's so elegant, so intelligent!" whooped Mrs. Blooper.

Immigration Officer Ellis wiggled her hips, clapped her hands, and exclaimed, "The Jedgar has pulled a Shakespeare!"

"We'll make him an honorary citizen of Paradise!" declared Mayor Mandher, wiping her tears on her hot-pink petticoat.

"It's a miracle!" proclaimed Reverend Saul L. O'Quease, Pastor of Saint William the Divine's.

As the words of the poem flew into her heart, Rosie grew starry-eyed. It was love at first sonnet.

But in an instant her mood changed, and she turned pink as the outfit she wore. She was center stage, and she knew it, and she'd give the folks a good show. She sprayed herself with perfume, curtsied to the crowd, and gaily quoted the Bard:

Our day of marriage shall be yours,
One feast, one house, one mutual happiness.

With those words, the official announcement was made, and the wedding invitations were out. The oldies burst into riotous applause and watched to see what she'd do.

"I'm coming!" shouted Rosie, skipping onto her windsurf.

With her red hair flying, her dimples dancing, and her aura as bright as could be, she tacked to the Inferno and the arms of her only love.

*

"My, my," said Marie Celeste, reading the society pages of The Elsinore X-Press. "Life is full of surprises. Very unsettling for those of us who wish to age gracefully."

"What's wrong, Aunt Marie Celeste?" asked Lindsey.

"My baby sister is going to marry Mr. J. Edgar Lectrolux next week. I wonder what the 'J' stands for. I always prefer to address people by their full names."

"It's the Jedgar."

Out of the force of habit, Marie Celeste arched an eyebrow. In polite circles it would take time before the J-word became fully acceptable.

"I know, my dear," she said. "I've just read the marriage banns. I suppose that as the older sister, it's my duty to put a stop to such nonsense."

"You're going to stop the wedding?"

"Heaven's no. Not the wedding, the *banns*. If you study your Shakespeare, you'll learn that it is never wise to obstruct true love."

Lindsey felt inexplicably relieved.

What now? she asked herself. She sensed that something was missing, and it dawned on her that she sorely needed some fun. She hadn't played tennis or gone sailing since she'd arrived, nor had she visited the amusement parks and the game sites.

As for the K⁴CC kids, in her opinion they were pretty awesome, and she hadn't had much of a chance to get to know them.

But she would. Summer wasn't over yet, and she was raring to get herself one whopping good vacation. She promised herself that while the oldies fussed around preparing for Rosie's wedding, she and the Rangers were going to have the time of their lives in the Pink Zone.

She suddenly noticed that her aunt hadn't stopped talking, and she tuned in to the tail end of the spiel.

"Remember, my dear, that every young woman has the right to marry the monster of her choice. And I must admit that my baby sister, foolish and unruly as she is, has demonstrated the good sense to reform the savage rather than accept him the way he was. If he can be civilized, anybody can. Always be open-minded, Lindsey. That's lesson number eleven."

"Did you ever marry, Aunt Marie Celeste?"

"I preferred not to. However, in theory, I have nothing against it. Education is my fortress against prejudice. When I was a small child, I read *Beauty and the Beast* several times."

"The Jedgar said you called him a non-person."

"Quite so. He displayed no human qualities. A monster lives only for what it wants, a person lives by ideals. You know, my dear," she confided, "I sometimes suspect that when Mr. Lectrolux was young, he watched too many violent movies."

Lindsey tuned out again and started daydreaming of the wedding. She wondered if her tailor-made dress could be ready in time. She also wanted to buy a nice present for the bride and groom.

"I don't know what to get them for a wedding gift."

"I'd suggest a picture of yourself. They're sure to be pleased. You look so much like Marie Rosette when she was twelve. I, personally, attach very little importance to appearances. What a young lady needs is character, and I must say that yours has improved greatly thanks to my etiquette lessons."

Lindsey knew she'd be in hot water if she mentioned her opinion of the etiquette lessons. Instead she asked, "You really think they'd like my picture?"

"Certainly. Why don't you go to Zee Rock's Reproductions and have one made? And while you're in town, please order my gift – that is if you don't mind missing the *Good Morning Elsinore show*."

"It's all right," said Lindsey. "What are you giving them?"

"Just what they'll be needing most," she replied sagely, "an S.O.S. 3000."

*

Lindsey called Ryan who called Oscar. In a three-way, walkie-talkie conference call, the boys cross-examined her on every detail of her kidnapping, and she was glad she'd picked the Jedgar's brain before she left.

"I'll meet you at Maxi's," she told them, readying herself to go out.

To her dismay, Marie Celeste nabbed her at the door and delayed her with a lecture on Bardolatry. Just as she was winding down, Lindsey made the mistake of asking what all the squabbling was about if everybody worshiped the same Bard.

"I'm pleased that you've finally asked," said the aunt. "As every true Elizabethan knows, the sublime Mr. Shakespeare, our inspiration and joy, has ennobled us through his works. While all Paradisians bow to his greatness, we differ about his voice. The enlightened Blues find his truth in Tragedy; the Pinks, in their frivolity, claim that Comedy is king. As for the waffling Whites, who cherish his historical plays –"

"A wedding is a happy ending," said Lindsey, her hand on the doorknob, "so it means the Pinks have won."

"Not yet, my dear," countered the aunt. "Comedy ends at the altar. In Tragedy, that's where it starts."

By the time Lindsey got out of the house, the Elsinore Rangers had already converged on Maxi's and were noisily discussing her adventure. As Lindsey swung through the revolving doors, excitement was ripe, and she found herself mobbed.

"She's here!" yelled Richie, tripping over Sherman, who groveled at his feet.

Cameras flashed, and the Rangers crowded around her firing questions. And Lindsey discovered how it feels to be a celebrity – for fifteen minutes.

"Lindsey, I've got to thank you. Your Aunt Rosie is a marvel," said Richie, tossing a peanut to Sherman. "She's got K⁴CC all sorted out."

"Sherman's stopped attacking?"

"Peaceful coexistence," he smiled. "Come on, Shermy, show her your new tricks."

"Lindsey, I'm so glad you're safe," said Cerise. "I'm fixing up new T-shirts for the wedding, and I'm putting that Jingle Bell poem on them. Can you help me –"

"Lindsey," cut in Jack, "is the Jedgar *really* J. Edgar Lectrolux?"

"Yes, and he's going to be *my* uncle."

"Wow!" exclaimed the wannabe secret agent. "He's my hero. I'd give anything to meet him. J. Edgar Lectrolux in person!"

"I'm not sure that's possible," she said, madly improvising. "Of course, the Jedgar gave *me* a tour of the control room. It's all done with mirrors."

"The control room!" he yelped. "Come on, give a guy a break. This might be my one chance in a lifetime."

Lindsey was beginning to enjoy herself at Jack's expense. "But the Jedgar is an honorable man. He'll be scandalized when he finds out you've been shaking us down like a thug!"

"The secret service doesn't hire weasels," added Ryan. "He'll probably see to it you never get a job."

Zach smiled broadly, "Tough luck, Squirt."

"Looks like you're all washed up, Jackie boy," said Chip.

"What if I return all the stuff I got?" Jack's complexion drained to a sickly gray. He removed his Electronic Epsilon Delux iiiWatch and handed it to Chip. "I'll give everything back today. I promise."

"I'll think about it," said Lindsey. "Cerise's canary better be in good shape."

"The mysteries seem to be solved," said Ryan. "Are there any questions left to clear up?"

"Just one," said Lindsey. "When are we going waterskiing?"

Ryan let off a whoop. "How about it, guys?" And for the first time all summer nobody needed any persuasion.

"Can't y'all tell me why there are so many blackouts?" asked Cerise, and Lindsey suggested she ask the Jedgar.

"Where did he get all the money to build the Inferno?" said Richie, impressed by such deep pockets.

Lindsey had asked the Jedgar that same question. "Federal grant," said she.

Zach said, "Is there an ice hockey match today?" When the Rangers all shook their heads, he pointed at the window and said, "So what's that?"

They stared out at a passerby muzzled in a head-hincher, which looked like a cross between a goalie's mask and a bird cage. Unable to believe their eyes, they rushed to the window and pressed their noses to the glass for a better look.

"It's my Uncle Jerry," said Ryan, cracking up, "in a Brace the Face Special with a triple Jerk the Jaw Jammer!"

"The poor old man," said Cerise.

The kids fell apart laughing. With peals and squeals of delight, they doubled over in convulsions and laughed uncontrollably until their sides ached. Even Sherman seemed to be chuckling.

"He looks like an extra-terrestrial!" hooted Oscar.

"Why would an oldie wear a contraption like that?" cried Richie, holding his stomach and laughing hilariously.

"His teeth!" howled Ryan, setting off another round of laughter. "He wants to get back into office!"

They laughed deliriously, the tears streaming down their cheeks, and they couldn't stop until they were so drained and winded and woozy for lack of air that they collapsed on the floor trying to catch their breath.

"What's so funny?" asked Cerise, beginning to giggle despite herself.

"Poetic justice," gasped Lindsey.

The belly-laugh served to remind them of their appetites. The occasion called for a feeding frenzy, and they all decided to splurge. They poured over the menu, marveling at the choices that peacetime had brought to Paradise.

They paged a dumbot and placed their orders: a jumbo Tex-Mex platter, two deep-fried chickens, two lasagnas, a baked stuffed lobster, a roast turkey dinner with all the trimmings, a vegetarian variety plate, and a steak sandwich – medium rare, plus side orders of potato frills, nachos, corn-on-the-cob, sunflower seeds, onion rings, hominy grits, apple fritters, fried clams, chef's salads, and piping hot muffins — plus a bucket of buttered popcorn for Sherman.

"I feel like celebrating," bubbled Cerise, clinking her glass of papaya punch against Rhett's. "Let's have another round of drinks!"

"What about the desserts?" asked the Jackerman.

"Oh, we won't forget the just deserts." Lindsey nodded to Ryan.

"Yeah," he shouted, gleefully snapping his fingers at the dumbot, "be sure to put everything on Jack's bill!"

*

"Lindsey! Pick up the phone. Your father's on the line."

"Yes, Aunt Marie Celeste."

She snatched the receiver. "Dad!"

"Hi, honey. I'm back in San Diego."

"With my new puppy?"

"Here's a little hint — there's a puddle on the kitchen floor."

"Whoopee! I can't wait to see him!"

"And me?"

"You too, Dad."

"Come on home, Globe-trotter. I miss you. I want to hear all about your trip."

"What about the wedding?"

"Lindsey, I don't want to upset you. We'll talk about it when you're here."

Something in his voice reminded her of somebody, but she couldn't think who.

"Out with it," she said.

"I know how attached you are to Tiffany, and I hate to disappoint you but –"

"You're *not* going to marry her!"

"Please don't sound so shocked, Lindsey. It's all for the best."

"Dad, I can't stand her."

"You can't?"

"I think she's an airhead."

"I'm so relieved," he chuckled, "but I wish you'd told me before. I was afraid you'd be upset."

All at once she knew who her dad sounded like. The discovery hit her with the voltage of an electrical power plant. He's exactly like *me*! Like father like daughter, what a pair of wimps! All we ever do is tiptoe around each other's feelings!

She wondered how it all had begun, but deep down inside she knew: the hurt that they'd never dealt with, the loss that they'd never faced. She suddenly felt like hugging him and making everything all right.

Poor dear old daddy, she sighed. He was the funniest, smartest, nicest father she could want, but maybe like the Jedgar, he sometimes needed a little help. She'd have to do something about it.

"Can I take an assertiveness training course when I get home?"

"I suppose so," he laughed. "We can decide later."

"If you really care about keeping me out of trouble, you'd better promise right now," she said.

Never had she sounded less like a wimp.

"I guess if you really want it that much, it's a promise."

"Did you find another girlfriend in Australia?"

"It's not what you're thinking...."

Here we go again, she thought wryly, but if it's another bimbo, he's going to hear about it. There were plenty of assertiveness training programs in San Diego. Lindsey would find one that offered a family plan.

"I'll be home right after Rosie's wedding," she said.

"Marie Rosette's getting married again? God bless her."

"I'll tell you all about it when I see you."

"I love you, Lindsey."

"Love you, too."

*

The matrimony of Ms. Marie Rosette O'Neill and Mr. J. Edgar Lectrolux was a splendiferous affair to out-sparkle all previous bashes. Pinks, Whites, and Blues showed up dressed in their fanciest finery with silken coats and caps and golden rings, with ruffs and cuffs and fardingales and things. So many people wanted to attend that they couldn't all fit into Saint William the Divine's, and the ceremony with all its niceties had to be transferred to the Globe Theater, the only venue large enough to hold the entire populace.

Usually reserved for the Shakespeare festival and other time-honored pageants, the Globe was an imposing, three-story, open-air amphitheater painted white with contrasting dark brown wooden beams. Never before had it been used for a wedding, however Reverend Saul L. O'Quease agreed to preside over the ceremony. By his side at the altar stood the Jedgar wringing his hands as he waited for the bride to appear.

At the bewitching twilight hour, the sky-blue-pink of the heavens morphed into a velvety violet backdrop, and a panoply of stars materialized to form a halo over Paradise. Suddenly a symphony of stringed instruments began to play the wedding march. Spotlights zeroed in on Rosie as she swept onto the stage, her hands gently folded around a pint-sized water bottle.

All eyes turned on her. She was perfectly ravishing in her imported Dolce & Stil Novo designer gown, and a flurry of whispers rippled through the stands.

"It's the wedding of the century," gushed Juanita Shringapur who, at the age of a hundred and fifty-three, remembered them all.

"She may be aging disgracefully," asserted Marie Celeste, a touch of undisguised pride in her voice, "but you can still tell she's an O'Neill. She looks as beautiful as a bride."

"As a bride," said Miss Prymm.

Mayor Mandher peered between the cleats of her husband's head-hincher until she found the eye-slots. She gazed through the narrow slits and smiled at him fondly.

"You know, Jerry," she said, "I may be just a silly old romantic, but I'm thrilled that they're finally getting married. Some things are just meant to be."

"Or not to be," he grunted.

As Rosie O'Neill glided by in glory, the guests tossed rice crisps at her feet. The orchestra switched to the Jedgar's favorite tune,

"My Wild Irish Rose," and an angelic, solo voice broke into song. Lindsey looked up and saw Cerise at the microphone singing:

> They may sing of their roses, which by other names,
> Would smell just as sweetly, they say.
> But I know that my Rose would never consent
> To have that sweet name taken away.
> Her glances are shy when e'er I pass by
> The bower where my true love grows,
> And my one wish has been that some day I may win
> The heart of my wild Irish Rose.
>
> My wild Irish Rose, the sweetest flower that grows.
> You may search everywhere, but none can compare
> [with my wild Irish Rose.
> My wild Irish Rose, the dearest flower that grows,
> And some day for my sake, she may let me take
> [the bloom from my wild Irish Rose.

At the sight of Rosie, the Jedgar added his tenor to the music. Soon everyone in the stadium was singing. They linked arms around each other's waists and swayed back and forth in unison. When the blushing bride reached the blushing groom, she set her water bottle on the altar and gave him a coquettish smile. Overjoyed, the Jedgar took her hand and pressed it to his lips.

With great pomp and fanfare, Reverend O'Quease opened his *Complete Works of William Shakespeare*.

"Before I sanctify this union and pronounce you man and wife, I would like to read a few words from our one and only Bard, in whose wisdom all Paradisians rejoice," he said in solemn devotion. He turned to the Jedgar and read:

> If by your art...you have
> Put the wild waters in this roar, allay them.
> The sky, it seems, would pour down stinking pitch …

The Jedgar bowed his head in shame. "I apologize for all the wrongs I've done, and I pledge to put a stop to earthquakes, floods, and all other unnatural disasters. There will be peace in Paradise."

Reverend O'Quease turned to Rosie and read:

> This above all—to thine own self be true,
> And it must follow, as the night the day,
> Thou canst not then be false to any man ...

"Aw, naw!" cried Rosie. She let go of the Jedgar's hand and burst out crying.

"What now?" asked Reverend O'Quease.

"You just made me remember. I can't marry him." Rosie pulled out her hankie and bawled.

"Aw, naw!" cried the Jedgar, blubbering over. He slumped to the floor and began hammering his head against the altar.

"Why can't you marry him?" demanded Reverend O'Quease.

"'Cuz of what the Bard said. Above all, I gotta be true to myself. And I wrote in my diary that I wouldn't marry him if he was the last person on earth."

"And she always keeps her word," moaned the Jedgar.

"A noble sacrifice," said Reverend O'Quease, but nobody heard him because the loud weeping of the bride and groom drowned him out.

The wedding guests were stunned, frozen into silence. Reverend O'Quease shut his book and turned to leave, shaking his head in defeat.

"Wait a minute!" cried Lindsey, the words bursting from her mouth. She jumped out of her seat and rushed up to the altar. "Rosie said she wouldn't marry him if he was the last person on earth, but he *isn't* the last person on earth, so she *can* marry him."

"Huh?" went Rosie.

"It's a syllogism," said Lindsey.

"I don't know anything about any silly gismo," said Rosie.

"It's logic," said Lindsey. "It's a way of using reason to find an answer."

"I don't understand one word you're saying. I want my Jedgar!" sobbed Rosie. And she stamped her foot.

"Logic isn't her strong point," groaned the Jedgar.

"Ryan, come here," called Lindsey. "Explain the syllogism so she can understand it."

"Here I am," he said, running up to join them. "Rosie, please try to concentrate."

She crossed her fingers and squinted her eyes.

"Now, who did you say you'd never marry?" asked Ryan.

"The Jedgar."

"Think again, Rosie. I want you to tell me the exact WORDS you put into your diary. WHO did you say you'd never marry?"

"The last person on earth," said she.

"The Jedgar isn't the last person on earth, is he?"

"No," agreed Rosie, thinking hard.

"So –" coaxed Ryan.

"So –" urged Lindsey.

"So –" pleaded the Jedgar.

Invisible light bulbs started flashing inside Rosie's brain.

"So," she laughed, "I can marry him."

And she did.

Chapter Nineteen

THIS OTHER EDEN, DEMI-PARADISE

Stars dimpled the cheek of night, and the band played on. Everybody frolicked into the wee small hours on the roller coasters and Ferris wheels and water slides near Rosie's tree house.

The wedding feast was a picnic barbecue, replete with anteaters that the groom had given the bride as a token of his affection. Rosie returned her gold earrings to the Jedgar, and she gave him a brand new squirt-gun, which he used to fill his mouth with Montezuma's Miracle Mineral. Then they cracked open crate upon crate, and the water flowed like champagne.

The dancing went on and on to beat the band as Captain Friedman's combo, known as Sammy's Swinging Songbirds, reveled to a feverish pitch. Cerise and Lindsey danced with every boy in Paradise except Zach, whom they took turns snubbing. When Zach finally gave up on them, he found a cute new girl to schmooze, and he danced cheek to cheek with her for twenty minutes before discovering she was a dumbot.

Ryan and the K⁴CC crew, who weren't much into dancing, soon tired of it and headed to the refreshment stand. And Jack, no longer in disgrace with fortune and men's eyes, followed the Jedgar around like a bloodhound until Cerise stepped to the rescue.

"Would you please dance with me, Mr. Jedgar?" she asked.

"Play it again, Sam," called the Jedgar, and the combo burst into another round of "My Wild Irish Rose."

"Lindsey, Ryan, come here," said Rosie. "My pal Eartha's back in town with her Rejuvenated Kit-Kat Show, and Kitsy's gonna be the star. Let's go find out when it starts."

"How about it, guys?" asked Ryan, but the K⁴CC kids nixed the idea. They'd already seen it and preferred to go down to the mini-golf.

Rosie slipped her arms through Lindsey's and Ryan's and led them away. Out of the corner of her eye, she spotted Jack and said, "Aren't you comin'?"

"Me?" It wasn't often that Jack was welcomed anywhere.

Rosie gave him a winning smile. "Sure thing. Don't wanna miss the purr-formance, do ya?"

After a moment's hesitation, Jack tagged along after them. And so did Zach, who always felt welcome everywhere.

Back on the dance floor, the waltz picked up, and the Jedgar gaily twirled Cerise through the crowd.

"ONE, two, three, ONE, two, three," counted the Jedgar, executing a clumsy box-step, his nose aimed at his feet.

"Can I ask a real serious question?" said Cerise.

"I'll answer anything you like if you'll sing for me again."

Cerise warbled like a nightingale, and he broke into a smile of sheer bliss. When the music stopped, she batted her eyes at him and asked, "How come there's so many blackouts?"

"Don't you know, my dear?" The Jedgar smiled benevolently. "Blackouts, quakes, tidal waves – there was nothing on earth I wouldn't do to get Rosie to notice me."

"Ahhh," sighed Cerise, at last content.

"And now it's time for some man-talk and some woman-talk. Please find Rosie and your Ranger friends and bring them to me."

Cerise searched the grounds and found Rosie, Ryan, Jack, Zach, and Lindsey, and she brought them back with her.

"These are the original Rangers," she told the Jedgar, "I can't find the K⁴CC boys. I've checked everywhere except the mini-golf."

"That's all right. These are the ones I wanted. I knew you'd bring the right ones."

"How did you know?" she asked.

"It's my business to know," said the Jedgar, and the Jackerman's heart palpitated in adoration.

"Rosie, my love, I'm taking the boys up to my studio for

some man-to-man talk. You take the girls for some woman-to-woman talk."

Rosie kissed her seventh husband on the nose. "Don't be gone too long, my Jedgar. I wanna dance some more. It's not like I get married *every* day."

*

The Jedgar tugged a branch, and a ladder made of vines dropped from the terrace of Rosie's tree house. He invited the three boys up to a pleasant bower, which he'd converted into an office shaded by heart-shaped leaves and great puffs of flowers, and he took his place on a frond-fitted hammock. The boys sat on mats at his feet.

"Boys," he said solemnly, "I don't want my words to ever leave this room." All three nodded their assent.

"I've got some things here that may interest you." He opened his right hand and exhibited the rosebud earrings. Then he opened his left and showed them a palm-sized instrument they'd never seen before.

"Rosie and I have decided to give these earrings to Lindsey. But only the four of us," he indicated Ryan, Zach, Jack, and himself, "will ever know the secret of the earrings. One of you boys will 'own' the secret, and be free to act on it however you choose, and the other two of you will be sworn to silence." The three boys looked up expectantly as the Jedgar went on.

"Let me explain. I'm a natural born nosy-body, a super-snoop, and from the moment I met Rosie I always wanted to know where she was. So I installed microscopic global-placer-tracer chips in the earrings and made her promise never to take them off. One earring gives the longitude, and the other gives the latitude. For the last sixty years, I've known exactly where she was, give or take half a mile or so. The margin of inaccuracy led to a minor miscalculation. I made a terrible error of mistaken identity, but that error turned out to be such a blessing that I've decided to leave the earrings exactly as they are."

He paused to see if the boys understood. They clearly did. He snapped his fingers, and a gorbot came running.

"Take these earrings down to Mrs. Lectrolux so she can give them to Lindsey," he said, "and get back here fast. Someone might start quoting Shakespeare, and I don't want to see you explode." The gorbot exited earrings in hand.

"Gotta get these creatures reprogrammed," muttered the Jedgar to himself. "Now boys," he continued, "this placer-tracer monitors the earrings. All you've got to do is switch it on, and you can locate the girl wearing them. And from now on, that girl will be Lindsey. What I'd like to know is if one of you would like to have the placer-tracer."

All three raised their hands.

"My, oh my," said the Jedgar. "She's just like Rosie. Well, I don't know you boys very well, so if you tell me your reasons for wanting the placer-tracer, perhaps it'll help me make a choice. Let's start with the oldest."

"I'm the oldest," said Zach. "And I want the placer-tracer 'cuz I'm crazy for Lindsey. I want her to be my girl."

"Mmmm," said the Jedgar. "It warms my heart to hear it. And who is the second oldest?"

"I am," said Ryan.

"Why do you want it?"

"Lindsey's my best friend – maybe my only friend," he added, glumly thinking that within days he'd be going into ninth grade, the littlest kid in a high school full of strangers. "I just want to know where she is."

"A fine reason, young man. And you, Jack?"

"Strictly business. I'm gonna be the greatest spy in the world, and I could use an agent like her on the West Coast."

"Very good, m'boy. Our country needs minds like yours."

The Jedgar scratched his head indecisively. "The way I see it, your motives are love, friendship, and a rewarding career – the three best things a person can live for. But who am I to play God with another man's life? You'll all be going home tomorrow, so I'll arrange an impartial contest at the airport. After all, character is destiny."

The Jedgar pulled a spyglass from under his vest and scanned the area until he spotted Rosie and the girls. "But this is my wedding night. Come on, boys, let's party!" cried the super-snoop, latching onto a branch and swinging away.

*

Rosie kicked off her sandals and sat Indian-style on the grassy hillside, chatting with Lindsey and Cerise.

"I'm sooo happy. I've finally got the only man I've ever really loved," said Rosie, hugging herself and bursting into Shakespeare:

> Merrily, merrily shall I live now
> Under the blossom that hangs on the bough.

"And," she went on, "the first thing I'm gonna do is redecorate that Inferno. We're renaming it Eden Isle and turning it into the best part of Paradise. I'm gonna plant eucalyptus trees all over and fill them with Koala bears. And we'll have flowers and animals and friends in every room. It'll take a while to get the place *livable*, but men like to be kept waiting."

"Might want to do something about the grackle birds," said Lindsey.

"I'll have 'em chirpin' at my window in no time," grinned Rosie. "Gonna show that sister of mine that Comedy is king — her and her fourteen minutes."

"It sounds like a dream," mused Cerise, feeding a mustard seed to her Birdie. She let it hop a little from her hand and with a silken thread plucked it back. "How come you waited so long to get married if he's your one true love?"

"Had to have him on my own terms. And I knew he'd come around if I stuck to my guns," said Rosie, squirting the air with rose-water. "I could never marry a man with no poetry in his heart. Gotta have standards. Just remember, girls, unlike tiglons or canaries, men have to be trained *before* you catch them."

"You had it figured out all along," concluded Lindsey.

"I've had that Jedgar figured out since seventh grade."

The gorbot loped over and remained standing at attention. "Whatcha doin' here, big boy?" asked Rosie. The gorbot handed her the earrings, and she passed them to Lindsey.

"Just in time. These are for you," she said.

"For me? Thank you," said Lindsey, putting them on. "They're beautiful."

"Sure they're pretty — pretty hard and pretty cold. Better to have warm fuzzies." She tweaked Kitsy's chin. "Oh, and Lindsey, if you ever feel the earrings vibrate, it means you're being monitored. And a woman doesn't have to tell *every*thing she knows," smiled Rosie. Mysteriously.

*

All of Elsinore showed up for the bon voyage party at the airport, now officially known as Tisquantum International. Ryan, Zach, Jack, Lindsey, Cerise, and Birdie were taking Marie Celeste's King Lear jet home together. With hugs and kisses, they made their farewells to their oldie friends and relatives. Yung Lu showed up with fortune cookies the size of footballs, and he passed them out to the Rangers. Cerise broke from the crowd and tossed her cookie into the air like a baton.

"Hey, y'all," she shouted. "Give me a 'P'!"

"Indeed," sniffed Marie Celeste.

But the Rangers all rallied. "P!" they shouted.

"Give me an 'A-R-A-D-I-S-E'!" Cerise was so carried away that she didn't even realize she'd spelled it correctly.

"A-R-A-D-I-S-E!" went the Rangers.

"What y'all got?"

"Paradise!"

"Let me hear it!"

"PARADISE!"

"Let's all cheer it!"

"PARADISE! HURRAY!"

The oldies clapped and stamped their feet. They tossed confetti and tooted their noise-makers – but not, by any means, the Chair of the Blue Party.

"Lindsey, I expect that this boisterous little exhibition may serve as your twelfth and final lesson," said she.

"What lesson, Aunt Marie Celeste?"

"All the world's a stage."

"Did Shakespeare say that?"

"Certainly. Never forget it, Lindsey. It is by far the most important lesson of all. *Au revoir*, my dear." She fluttered her fingers, blew her grandniece an airy kiss, and with Miss Prymm at her heels performed a perfectly graceful exit.

The Jackerman rolled his eyes at his brother and snickered, "Yeah, sure, if the whole world's a stage, who's watching the show?"

The question hung in the air, but Cerise didn't miss a beat. "God is," she answered with a sunny smile. "He's watching all the time."

Lindsey felt a grin spreading across her face. She glanced at Ryan and saw that he was grinning too.

"Come on," she said to Ryan and Cerise. "Let's say good-bye to the K⁴CC crew."

They cut through the crowd, leaving the Bond brothers behind, and spent their curtain-call moments exchanging tongue-tied promises and heartfelt sentiments interrupted by bouts of embarrassed laughter. They all felt awkward and inexpressively profound — as befits the sweet sorrow of parting.

"Clear the runway!" barked Dogberry.

The electric blue King Lear jet taxied into position. Captain Friedman signaled from the cockpit, and the five departing Rangers headed for the plane.

"One moment, boys, it's time for our little test," said the Jedgar, calling back Ryan, Zach, and Jack. He turned to Mrs. Lectrolux. "Rosie, would you please get our hot air balloon ready? I'm taking you home as soon as I wind up a piece of unfinished business."

"Certainly, my love," she said, and off she skipped.

The Jedgar snapped for a gorbot and then addressed the three boys. "I've chosen a disinterested referee to conduct the contest for the placer-tracer, and I'll leave each of you to determine your own fate." He gave the small instrument to the gorbot and stepped aside. "It will belong to the one who can get it from the gorbot. Good luck to you all. It's been a pleasure meeting you, and may the best man win."

He shook hands with the boys and bounded off to join Rosie.

The gorbot held the placer-tracer over its head, and Zach, by far the tallest, jumped for it. Jack tried climbing up the grizzly leg. When the gorbot brushed him aside, he pulled its tail until the creature howled. Ryan scooted up the stairs, took a headlong leap at the gorbot's paw, and landed flat on his face.

Jack whispered to his brother, "Humpty Dumpty had a great fall!"

"Humpty Dumpty? So, *that's* his nickname!" snorted Zach.

"Shut up," said Jack, afraid that Ryan might overhear.

But Ryan had heard. Trembling all over, he picked himself up, and Jack tried to shove him down again.

"Let's use Fatso as a springboard," he said, and the Bond boys moved in on Ryan.

"No way!" yelled Ryan, making for the stairs.

Zach and Jack fixed their attention on the gorbot. They rushed at it together trying to tackle it like two linebackers felling a full-back, but the ape was prepared for them and much too bulky to knock over.

From the top of the staircase, Ryan observed the performance. As he watched them grunt and sweat, swatted around by the gorbot, he thought they looked like a pair of clowns. They seemed so puny and ridiculous and insignificant that he realized — to his astonishment — that he no longer cared what they called him. It meant nothing.

In a single moment, as if shedding a heavy coat at the first sign of spring, he felt a weight slipping from his shoulders, and he began to feel pretty darn good.

Suddenly his eyes lit up, and he declaimed:

> All that glitters is not gold;
> Often you have heard that told.

Many a man his life hath sold
But my outside to behold.

The gorbot emitted a ghastly roar and staggered backwards. It flipped head over heels three times and landed on its back. The placer-tracer flew through the air. Ryan stuck out his hand, caught it, dropped it into his pocket, and ran giggling into the plane.

*

"Ryan," said Lindsey, unfastening her seatbelt just before take-off. "Save my seat. I'm going up front. There's something I want to ask Captain Friedman."

"Wait a sec," he said, and he handed her the placer-tracer.

"What's that?" she asked, turning it over in her palm.

"A relic."

"Huh?"

"A souvenir of Jedgar mentality," he grinned. "Long story. I'll tell you later."

"Hey, Lindsey, why doncha sit with me?" asked Zach, edging his brother aside to take a leather chair. He sank into it and patted the armrest for Lindsey to sit on.

Lindsey smiled sweetly, opened the instrument panel, and hit "Rolling Massage," the "Maximum Extra High" button. Then she tapped on the cockpit door and stepped through just as she heard Zach yell, "Yikes!"

*

"Lindsey, glad you came forward," said Captain Friedman. "I thought you might be having too good a time with your friends back there." He dabbed his eyes with a tissue.

"You all right?" she asked.

"I'm just being sentimental. Young lovebirds always move me to tears."

He pointed out the window. Rosie and the Jedgar were standing on the runway holding hands and waving. In the background, Mount Cinderella was placidly blowing heart-shaped clouds toward heaven.

"They're not young," said Lindsey.

"They are on Paradise. Remember?"

"Captain Friedman, I'd like to ask you something. It's about me and the Rangers. Can we come back and live here when we turn seventy?"

"Sure. You're already on the waiting list. But you'd better send Marie Celeste a thank-you note. She cares about things like that. She might even invite you for your next school vacation."

"Mmmm," said Lindsey, thinking that she wouldn't turn thirteen until July, and there were several school vacations coming up before then. But even the winter break seemed quite far off. More so than that, she realized that she'd changed inside. Something told her that her life was about to start moving in a brand new direction.

The little globe-trotter felt serene. She was glad to be going home, and she couldn't wait to see her father and her friends and her puppy, her very own little dog. She wondered if Marie Celeste would let her bring a dog along on the next trip — maybe if she could train him to put up with a few etiquette lessons and lots of soft food.

Oddly, while Lindsey wasn't ready to plan four months in advance, her imagination had no problem skipping fifty-eight years at a leap.

"Might be kind of sad when I'm seventy," she said, voicing her concern. "I mean, when I get back, some of my oldie friends might not be here anymore."

"Why not? We take trips all the time, but none of us are planning to move away. Likely you'll find us all the same as ever when you come."

"Everybody? My aunts and the Jedgar too?"

"Of course. They're only in their early seventies. They have plenty of good years ahead. When you're seventy, they'll just be around a hundred and thirty. And by then the life expectancy should be much, much longer."

"And Yung Lu?"

"He's already planning his two-hundredth birthday," said the captain, opening the closet to check his co-pilot.

All at once, Lindsey felt worlds better, lighthearted and care-free. She gazed out the window at the bride and groom and waved merrily.

Still hand in hand, Rosie and the Jedgar hopped into the bas-ket of their hot air balloon. The last thing that Lindsey saw on Paradise was the happy couple floating through a heart-shaped cloud up to the sky together.

T'was a magic moment indeed – he with a sonnet in his heart and she with a syllogism in her head. They had been apart way too long, for no rhyme or reason.

Appendix

SOURCES

WILLIAM SHAKESPEARE

Tragedies: *Hamlet, Julius Caesar, King Lear, Macbeth, Othello, Romeo and Juliet, Titus Andronicus*

Histories: *Richard II*

Comedies: *All's Well that Ends Well, As You Like It, Love's Labour's Lost, The Merchant of Venice, The Merry Wives of Windsor, A Midsummer-Night's Dream, Much Ado about Nothing, The Taming of the Shrew, The Tempest, Twelfth-Night, The Two Gentlemen of Verona, The Winter's Tale*

Sonnets: *18, 29*

OTHER POETS

Maya Angelou, Matthew Arnold, Elizabeth Barrett Browning, Samuel Taylor Coleridge, Billy Collins, T. S. Eliot, Robert Frost, Louise Gluck, Homer, Patrick Kavanaugh, Henry Wadsworth Longfellow, Amy Lowell, Daniel X. O'Neil, Christina Rossetti, Carl Sandburg, Sappho, Walt Whitman, William Wordsworth, W. B. Yeats

SONGS

"Jingle Bells" by James Pierpoint
"My Wild Irish Rose" by Chauncey Olcott

About

THE AUTHOR
&
THE ILLUSTRATOR

Elizabeth Wahn's catchy jingles about her teachers used to send her classmates into gales of laughter and land her in the principal's office. After becoming a teacher herself, she used her knack for whipping up fun to instill a love of Shakespeare in her students. Born and raised in Boston, she spent her summers at her grandparents' home in Puerto Rico and grew up speaking Spanish and English. A graduate of Newton College (now part of Boston College) and Middlebury College, she has taught secondary school in Massachusetts, Luxembourg, and Rome. Always ripe for fun and adventure, she has visited almost a hundred countries with her husband. *Lindsey and the Jedgar* is her first book.

Ivy Steele was born and grew up in a small village in Southeastern England. College and a rewarding management career in London were followed by many years as a roving expatriate wife and mother of three, living in five countries and traveling to more than forty. Her children now far-flung, she and her husband currently reside in Rome. When, on impulse, she took up drawing she had no idea that art would turn into a passion. Foreign travel and extended stays in remote areas remain large in her life and provide continued inspiration for her artwork. Indeed, almost all of the drawings for *Lindsey and the Jedgar* were done during trips to Ethiopia. The image of Ryan was modeled on a boy from the rainforest area near the Sudanese border.

To send a note to
Lindsey's author:

email: Wahn@LindseyandtheJedgar.com

Lindsey
and The
Jedgar
Website

www.LindseyandtheJedgar.com

Made in the USA
San Bernardino, CA
08 October 2013